DRIFTWOOD SPRINGS

A DONATELLA NOVEL

DEMETRIUS JACKSON

ACKNOWLEDGMENTS

I owe a huge thank you to everyone who supported me as this book made its way to market. Especially my first set of beta readers, Paul Colon, Rebecca Cannon, Katrina Sardis, and Reggie Richardson. Your insight was invaluable.

DEDICATION

Tarrance, Jasmyn, and Bryce. The three of you are the foundation that grounds me and keeps me going.

PROLOGUE
TUESDAY, SEPTEMBER 17TH – 10:00 A.M

With ragged breathing and a shivering body, the limp form struggled to keep the threadbare blanket over a lanky body. Enveloped by darkness with the only illumination coming from the yellowing light at the end of the corridor, the enclosure was both damp and windowless. In these surroundings it was nearly impossible to keep track of time, and the occupant could not tell if it was day or night. The predicament grew worse by the minute, as every third breath brought forth an accompanying cough. No longer covering the mouth with each cough as had been learned from a young age, the figure said aloud and to no one in particular, "HEY YOU! Let me out of here! Let me out of -"

A wheezing, coughing fit brought the demands to an abrupt end. Bleak understanding reared its head yet again as the figured realized the prospect of leaving this place anytime soon was remote. Curling knees to chest and wrapping arms around legs underneath the see-through blanket, the figure amended that previous thought. *I'm never going to leave this place – alive.*

1

FRIDAY, SEPTEMBER 13TH – 7:00 P.M

"Let me pour my heart through my chest."

"Lawd! Here we go again."

"These feelings that I feel puts my pen to the test. Memories that I have lays my soul down to rest."

"Marcellous, my ears are about to bleed."

"Visions of our union here dwells the real quest. Proceed with the rest, the truth is I miss."

"You know what I miss? My sanity! You sound like two cats fighting in the alley on a hot summer day dying of thirst!"

"Jasmyn, there is no need to be a sideline hater. I have a voice made of pure gold. Heck, had I been alive during the 70's I would have been a Motown legend."

"Yeah hon, a legend in your own mind. Do I need to bring to your selective recollection the cruise karaoke debacle of 2017? I have firmly implanted in my mind the blank stares and looks of horror as you screeched through 'Can You Stand the Rain'?"

"What did they know? They were not true judges of

vocal excellence. And if I recall correctly, I received a standing ovation."

"One person standing, an ovation does not make! And if I recall correctly, she stood to help point you off of the stage. Babe, we all have our shortcomings, and holding a note, any note, is certainly one of yours."

"There is a comedian in every family, and you my dear have found your calling."

"Just stating the facts!"

Continuing their drive home, the sun begins to descend in the west, illuminating the fall leaves a trio of burnt orange, fiery red, and a hint of Tuscan sun yellow. Distant sounds of birds chirping ride the waves of the wind through the open windows, serenading their ears. Marcellous glances over at his bride of three years and swells inside with the love he's had since the day he first met her many years ago.

The two had an auspicious beginning. Marcellous, rushed to the hospital after taking several gunshots during an apparent robbery, had to go through extensive rehab in order to regain full motor control. Prior to the shot that nearly paralyzed Marcellous, he had been a star basketball player at his university. Although his childhood had seen many trials and tribulations, he overcame each of them. With the support of his adopted family and his drive to succeed, he was able to persevere.

Jasmyn was a nursing student when she met Marcellous. Working as an aide to the head nurse, she was responsible for his rehab, which had him sulking and fighting her every step of the way. There were days that she managed only ten productive minutes in their one-hour session, yet she was determined to see him succeed. After two weeks of constantly nagging him to take his rehab seriously, Marcellous asked her out. No bravado was in his request, and she could tell he was sincere. If one had to describe the request, he'd asked with a shy, almost uncertain voice.

She thought he was cute and filled with unlimited potential, yet he was still a patient, and that was a line she would not cross. However, he pressed and pursued, and a deal was struck. "If you conclude your rehab and become discharged from my care, then and only then will I consider meeting you for coffee," she told him.

That seemed to be the kick in the pants he needed to become a model patient. Marcellous attacked his rehab with a singular determination to have that coffee, even though he never drank the stuff. For a chance to be in the presence of Jasmyn's graceful elegance, he would finish rehab and seize his opportunity.

Turning to face Marcellous, Jasmyn replayed the memory of their wedding day. He looked perfect standing at the altar with his best man. His eyes gleamed when the church doors swung open to reveal his bride in her wedding dress. The fear she held close that she would never meet her soulmate. The fear she would wake up to find this was a sick, twisted joke and by the time she reached the altar, she would awake. She stared at him, remembering the vows they spoke. The silky tone in his voice when he said, "I do." The preacher announcing them husband and wife and smiling before announcing, "You may kiss your bride."

It was not a dream! It was her reality. She was now Mrs. Jasmyn Thompson. As they hopped over the broom and made their way past the friends and family who had gathered to celebrate their union, she was happy. A happiness she had not envisioned. A happiness she would not relinquish for any reason in the world.

Ascending the final hill leading to their subdivision, tucked away in the suburbs of Charlotte, North Carolina, Jasmyn was startled from her trance by Marcellous's expletive.

"What in the hell is going on here?"

Peeling her eyes from her husband's chiseled yet stoic face, Jasmyn noticed the barricade leading to their gated community in Driftwood Springs. The gate was being manned by a thirty-ish-year-old woman from the local police department. Behind her were a series of police cruisers and one news van already on the scene.

Waiting in line behind two other cars, Jasmyn began to speak.

"My word! What could be causing this much commotion?"

"I don't know, babe! From the looks of it something serious has transpired in our little slice of heaven."

"Maybe the neighbors heard you singing in the shower and had enough."

"Ha ha ha! You know, you don't sing all that well yourself." Marcellous knew that was a lie. His wife had one of the most mesmerizing voices he had ever heard in his life, but she always refused to sing on request for total strangers. From the scene that unraveled in front of them, they could see the occupants in the car handing items over to the policewoman.

"They are not playing around," Jasmyn stated. "Whatever it is, they seem to have the entry to the neighborhood locked down tight."

Next in line, Marcellous pulled his vehicle five inches away from the officer, looked over at Jasmyn with a "here goes" shrug, and rolled down the window. When the officer leaned over the frame of the car, Marcellous could see up close the lovely look she had about her. He thought, *she's stunning for an enforcer of the law*. She had bluish-green eyes that could pierce the soul and quicken the rhythm of the heart. Eyes that seemed to smile as he gazed into them, which at the same time demanded the respect that came with the badge. She had dirty-blonde hair straightened and slightly hugging the contours of her heart-shaped face. From the full body of her lips to the slightly bronzed tan of her skin, delving deep into her family ancestry would be intriguing and enlightening.

"Good evening, we're validating all entries into the community. Please provide your license for verification."

Reaching into his front pocket to retrieve his wallet, Marcellous inquired, "Why the commotion this evening, Officer... Lewis?" He noticed the name on her badge affixed to her shirt.

Fighting to procure his license from the plastic clear window of his wallet, he heard Officer Lewis respond. "An eleven-year-old boy has gone missing."

"Missing!" exclaimed Jasmyn as her hand shot to her heart in an involuntary movement, and horror overtook her facial expression.

"Yes, missing. He was last seen leaving a neighbors' home where he and his friend were playing basketball. He texted his parents advising them he was on his way home – that was roughly two hours ago. When he didn't arrive as expected, his parents sent a follow-up text inquiring about the delay. When he didn't respond to their text, his mother called his phone – still no answer. Worried but not yet frantic, they called the home of his friend. The father confirmed he had left there around 5:00 p.m and figured he was already at home. Shortly thereafter a call was made to our precinct, and here we are."

With his license now free and his mind racing, Marcellous asked, "Whose boy is it?"

Glancing over the license and then back at Mr. Thompson, Officer Lewis stated, "It's the Grant family on Franklin Lane. Their son, Thomas, has disappeared."

"My God, Marcellous! That is very close to where we live. That poor family. They must be mortified." Jasmyn began to ponder incessantly. Although they didn't have any children, if this could happen to the Grant's, in this, their secure community, was it safe to even consider bringing children into this dark world? Was it worth the constant struggle between letting children be free and insulating them in a protective bubble? Was it worth the aging one endures when a teenager goes out with friends and the parents wait anxiously until they arrive home safely? Praying for that key to turn in the lock instead of doorbell ringing with an officer out front confirming their worst fears.

Officer Lewis handed Marcellous his license and urged the couple to proceed forward.

Finding her voice, she said, "Marcellous, this is unconscionable. I don't recall meeting the Grant's, but they are our neighbors, and we should stop by to see if there is anything that we can do to assist."

Marcellous, an introvert at heart, was not one to fraternize too much with the neighbors. He was always cordial and would speak with anyone when engaged. He had mastered the art of small talk that expanded beyond the normal talk of weather and work. While he didn't often engage in conversations with the neighbors at social community functions, he touted a keen sense of observation. He could discern and retain small details from their interactions and their lives that he could use in a pinch to bridge the conversation until he could exit gracefully.

"I don't know, babe," Marcellous stated. "This is an excruciatingly rough time for their family. I'm not sure they will want to have people prying around."

"If this happened to one of our children, wouldn't you want the community pulling together to assist where they could?"

"We don't have any children."

"No, we don't, and that's not the point. If we had children, we would want all the help our neighbors could muster in order to get our child back."

Inside, Marcellous knew she was right. If their not-yet-conceived child had gone missing, he would want the community, the city, heck the whole state, searching until their child was returned to them safe and sound. However, during one of the neighborhood's social functions, Marcellous witnessed something about Mrs. Grant. Something he had not shared with anyone, not even his wife. He began to contemplate if her secrets could have been the cause of their son's disappearance.

The two continued to wind their way through the subdivision. Careful to obey the "Keep our children safe. Speed Limit 20 mph" sign. Going agonizingly slow in his opinion, Marcellous mused internally, *Keep our children safe. Some bang up job they were doing at the moment.* Chastising himself for that thought, he turned the corner to Franklin Lane and was greeted with several other families from the subdivision who obviously had the same thought as Jasmyn.

A large group had already gathered, and the crowd continued to swell. Both sides of the street were lined with cars, while others opted to arrive by foot. Finding a parking spot at the T-Junction of Franklin and Patterson, Marcellous began the parallel parking maneuver he mastered as a Driver's Ed student while back in high school.

Coming flush with his back bumper to the back bumper of the lead car, Marcellous turned the steering wheel 270 degrees and slightly depressed the accelerator. The twin motors of his Tesla Model S gave that satisfying electric whine as the front bumper of his car began to slide past the back bumper of the car in front. At that moment, Marcellous rotated the steering wheel in the opposite direction as the car began to align within the proffered space. One final turn to straighten the wheels and, "Perfect!" he exclaimed.

"Yeah, like Officer Lewis?" Jasmyn inquired with a raised eyebrow and a smirk on her sensually brown lips.

"What?"

"Oh, I noticed you noticing her. No need to deny it."

"But, umm," stammered Marcellous.

"It's cool, love. She was kind of cute. But for the record, you're not leaving this subdivision again until she is off duty."

"Yes ma'am!" Marcellous chuckled as he pushed the button on the gear selector to place the car in park.

"I wondered," Jasmyn continued. "What would cause someone to kidnap their child? Think about it. According to Officer Lewis, this happened over two hours ago. For goodness' sake, it was still daylight hours. And you mean to tell me no one saw or heard anything? That seems awfully strange to me. You would think someone would have seen or heard something. You want me to believe no one heard a child scream?"

"Unless Thomas knew the person who kidnapped him." Marcellous said without hesitation.

"You must be kidding!" Jasmyn exclaimed. "Who does he know who would want to kidnap him?"

"I'm not saying that is what happened. I'm just merely suggesting that if no one heard him scream, which you would assume he would have done if he was being abducted, then he likely trusted the person who has him now."

"I don't know, Marcellous. That assertion sounds fragile to me. Someone would need a reason to kidnap him if he was known by the assailant. What would the motive be?"

Marcellous knew his logic faltered on slippery slopes. As he started to visualize the secrets that people kept, and how some of those indiscreet moments in the dark can lead to devastating consequences, he said, "I don't know, Jasmyn. Let's go see how we can lend a hand."

2
FRIDAY, SEPTEMBER 13TH - 7:30 P.M
GRANT RESIDENCE (735 FRANKLIN LANE)

With the sun tucked firmly behind the clouds and day folding into night, a plethora of concerned neighbors piled onto Franklin Lane hoping to ascertain the whereabouts of young Thomas Grant. Young kids filled with nervous energy and under the watchful gaze of their parents ran around carefree and oblivious to the seriousness of the night. Some older girls in the neighborhood began lighting candles and muttering speculations as to what may have transpired.

"I heard he ran away," chattered one of the girls. "I mean, think about it. When your dad is a tech billionaire, people see you as dollar signs – even those you consider friends. That likely drove him over the top."

"I heard," another girl started up, talking over the first. "I heard that he used some of his daddy's money to fly in one of those mail order brides from Russia, and that he was going to meet her for a quick tryst."

Meanwhile, the older boys filled with bravado and

camaraderie for a lost friend described in detail what they would do to the person who took Thomas.

"My dad keeps his Mossberg 500 Pump-Action shotgun locked away in his gun cabinet. He thought he did a good job of disguising the key's hidden location, but there are only so many places it could be hidden for quick access. Once I thought through the locations, finding the key was a cinch. Anyway, I'd blow the face right off of that son of a bitch without a second thought!"

"Seriously, Jeffery? You've never even shot a gun and more than likely would hit one of us instead of the culprit. Me on the other hand, I'm a proficient sniper with a crossbow and have finished first in our Boy Scouts archery competition two years in a row. I've had my eye on the Killer Instinct Ripper 415 Crossbow for the last year. This is the perfect time to convince my dad to drive me to the store to make my purchase. Then the hunt begins. When I find him, it'll be one in the groin, because obviously he's a sick bastard, and then one in each kneecap. That fucker will never sire kids or walk again."

Closer toward the house, the scene was quite different. Two police cruisers parked parallel to the circular path leading to the Grant's front door. In the courtyard, with the fall wind perceptibly cooler and nightfall on the horizon, they formed a search party.

"We have roughly sixty minutes before the sun fully sets," said one of the men.

Leaning closer to his wife's ear, Marcellous whispered, "Who is that guy?"

With the look of amusement and a trace of sarcasm, Jasmyn shook her head and asked, "Do you remember any of our neighbors? Geez Marcellous, get it together. Anyway, that is Brian Lawson. His wife and three kids live at the house on the corner of Franklin and Rose Street. If I recall correctly their address is 2800 Rose St. Their middle daughter, Sara, is in the same class as Tommy, and they have been friends since preschool. I'm sure this is hard on her, which is probably why her dad has taken a keen interest in leading this search party."

"Be sure to carry an extra set of batteries for your flashlights and search in pairs." Brian carried on in his authoritative voice. "No clue is too small and should not be discounted. You never know what could lead to the successful recovery of young Tommy. If you find anything, be sure to broadcast your findings over the walkie-talkies. We will use channel four for our communications, and this line is to stay open at all times. By that I mean no idle chit-chattering. We have already lost an hour pulling this party together. Make final preparations and we head out in five minutes."

The tension in the group was almost suffocating. The prevailing unspoken collective thought of the group, *this could be my child*, electrified the air. When faced with such a stark revelation, it changes a person. Every man and woman had taken on an entirely new perspective. The security provided by the gate now seemed to be a lie in advertisements and was now replaced with indescribable fear in the present.

A couple in their mid 40's made eye contact with the Thompson's. A look of curiosity and a lack of recognition marred their facial features.

The woman, a little portly, stood about 5 foot 3 with fleshy ankles and hands that looked like they could rip a lobster in half with minimal effort. She had a tangled mess of auburn hair and glasses with square frames that continued to slide to the bridge of her nose. She dressed in the latest fashions, though a little snug in the waist, and continued to exude the *don't mess with me* resting bitch face.

The man in contrast was roughly 5 foot 8 with broad shoulders. His frame comically continued narrowing down to his feet. In the right light he could be mistaken for an inverted life-size Spinning Top. He dressed in an orange and green Adidas track suit with matching shoes. He wore his hair close to his scalp and looked as if his nose had seen the wrong side of too many bar fights.

The woman, keeping eye contact with Marcellous and Jasmyn, stood up on her tip toes to speak with the man, presumably her husband. He nodded his head in a form of affirmation, and the two began sauntering over to make contact with the Thompson's.

Pushing her glasses back to rest on her reddening cheeks the woman spoke, "Well, hello you two. I don't think I have ever seen you in our exclusive gated community. Who are you here visiting?"

Staying level in his tone, Marcellous said, "We are not visiting anyone in this, our exclusive gated community."

The man's eyebrows furrowed momentarily and with a jolt stated, "You're the new help for the Grant's. We hadn't had a chance to meet you yet. Terrible, just terrible this thing that has happened to their young lad. Do you have any ide-"

Cutting him off mid-sentence, Jasmyn said, "Sir, we are not the help for the Grant's. Matter of fact we aren't the help for anyone. We reside in this, with her hands she made quoting gesture three times 'exclusive gated community'. Now if you'll excuse us, I don't hear anyone calling our name, but I'm sure our time can be spent better elsewhere."

The woman pushed her glasses back from the tip of her nose and stood mouth agape, cheeks now a fire red, as Jasmyn and Marcellous casually walked away.

Friday September 13th – 7:50 p.m
MacManus Residence (237 Downs Lane)

SALVATORE "SAL" Grandson gave up the lights, camera, and action of New York City, and moved down to Charlotte, NC where he plans to retire. While in New York, Sal worked for the New York Daily News. In his time with the New York Daily, he did okay. Many of his stories were above the fold on the front page, but none garnered him the coveted prize of many journalists, the Pulitzer. And for Sal, this was okay. He always said he wasn't in the industry to win a prize but to keep integrity and honesty in his reporting. If he won the prize, great. He would accept it gratefully and get back to work. To him, he didn't need this award to validate him, his work, or the merits of the story that needed to be told. At least, this is what Sal continued to tell himself.

In the back of his psyche, that desire to stand amongst some of the greatest journalistic minds across the nation and to be recognized as the best for that year was burning ever so bright. He was certainly competitive. When it came to the story, nothing would stand in his way. He believed in reporting the facts and nothing but the facts, though there were times he bent the rules slightly to gain the upper hand on his competition. Especially that weasel Jane Markowitz with the Times.

She did her best to upstage Sal, even resorting to unscrupulous tactics. Once she paid a local kid five bucks to release the air from his front tires so she could scoop him on a story. Sal needed to hail a cab during rush hour in the Bronx and then fight the endless traffic. Traffic that materialized between the time he should have left in his car and the time he did leave in the cab thirty minutes later. Once he arrived at the scene, it was too late to generate the story in time for the evening edition. Jane became the toast of the town, though only for that week, and he had to sit back and watch her soak it all in like a sponge to water. He decided right then and there, no more sleeping with the enemy during the work week. *Though in journalism, aren't we always working,* he mused.

And Jane, now sworn enemies, would still stop by from time to time. Hell, who was he kidding? He knew if she were ever ready to settle down, he would have been that lion ready to pounce.

"That's the past," he said slightly under his breath. "I'm here and she's there. Time to move on."

"Excuse me?" Carmen said, turning her head slightly to the left and giving Sal that quizzical stare.

Awakening from his trance, Sal shifted in her direction. "I said, this is a beautiful house you have here. So big and with such nice, plush grass. I could never afford a place like this."

Dale MacManus, nibbled his wife's earlobe, prompting her to giggle like a teenage schoolgirl, then said, "Sal you should have hoped on the Orbitz stock when I told you. You'd be right here with us."

Dale and Sal knew each other from their days in New York. He was one of the top traders on the New York Stock Exchange. He had a feeling about Orbitz when their shares were trading at $3.33 per share. At the time he had an extra $20K sitting around, so he decided he was going big or going home. He purchased just over 6,000 shares. Two years later the stock was trading at $250 per share netting Dale nearly $1.5 million.

"Yeah, yeah, yeah," Sal said, shrugging his shoulders and turning his palms to the sky. "I told you I don't trust that voodoo magic you guys in the stock market perform. I like to keep my money where I can see it! Anyway, it was great visiting with you two again. You guys are coming to my house next weekend for brats and beers, right?"

"You know it!" Dale said, giving his friend a hug while Carmen opened the door. As Sal leaned in to give Carmen a kiss on the cheek, the faint sound of an approaching helicopter whipped through the air.

"I wonder what that is all about," said Carmen as she leaned in to receive the kiss from Sal.

"I don't know." The hairs on the back of Sal's neck began to stand. "But I'm certainly going to find out."

With the pleasantries behind them and his radar for news now on high alert, Sal hopped in his car and began driving towards the entrance of Driftwood Springs. Creeping closer to the gate he realized that there were a number of police personnel checking patrons as they entered the community. *Could something be going on inside of Driftwood Springs?*" As he formulated this thought, he realized the sound of the helicopter seemed to be centered on this community. Surveying the scene more closely, he also noticed a number of news vans lining up outside the gate.

A gleeful feeling of being an insider while they were on the outside brought a smile to his face.

However, there was no time to gloat. Sal needed to determine the source for this flurry of activity and thus the genesis of his story. He pulled in behind a blue Tesla Model S making its way deeper into the community. He had to admit, that was a gorgeous car and one day if – when - he won a Pulitzer, he would pick one up for himself.

Sal sensed the car was heading in the right direction, as there was a congregation of people descending on a particular location. He wasn't sure where this train would stop, but he was determined to ride it to the bitter end. When the car in front of him executed a perfect parallel parking job, he found a spot. The occupants, a male and a female, who he figured were married stepped out of the vehicle; Sal did the same. It was clear the mass of humanity had a destination in mind, and he settled in for the walk. The walk however wasn't a long one. All traffic seemed to stop at 735 Franklin St. A shrine of bears, hearts, and candles had been erected around the yard, and there were a number of people working to organize a search. Though the details were fuzzy, Sal was able to deduce a child was missing, *hence the reason for the helicopter*, he thought to himself.

Wandering around the perimeter, Sal wanted answers, but he also didn't want to alienate this community that was missing a child. He did his best to make his way closer to the front door without necessarily being at the absolute front. At some point an officer would be by to see the family, *if they aren't already here*. He'd see if he could wiggle some answers from the police without raising suspicions. Within the ambient noise he heard a conversation brewing that piqued his interest.

"Well, hello you two. I don't think I have ever seen you in our exclusive gated community. Who are you here visiting?" he heard a woman ask.

Had another journalist made their way inside the gate as well?

"We are not visiting anyone in this, our exclusive gated community." He heard a male voice reply. At this he turned so that he could get a better view of the individuals speaking. He immediately noticed it was the couple he was following in the blue Tesla.

"You're the new help for the Grant's. We hadn't had a chance to meet you yet. Terrible, just terrible this thing that has happened to their young lad..." *Oh boy*, he thought while registering the name Grant. This might turn ugly quick.

"Sir, we are not the help for the Grant's. Matter of fact we aren't the help for anyone. We reside in this exclusive gated community. Now if you'll excuse us, I don't hear anyone calling our name, but I'm sure our time can be spent better elsewhere," the wife said.

Good for you, Sal thought. "I like those two," he said to no one in particular. Thanks to their conversation, he now knew the missing child belonged to the Grants.

Ten minutes later another police cruiser showed up at the home of the Grants. This one appeared to hold the detective who was in charge of the case. Sal needed to think fast if he wanted teeth to this story he had percolating in the recesses of his mind. As the detective lifted himself out of the squad car, Sal knew his time was running short, and he would need to make a decision – soon.

"Officer," Sal started as the detective made his way toward the door. "Is it true the Grant kid has been kidnapped? We are all just so worried and want to ensure the rest of the children are not in any immediate danger."

This seemed to gain the attention of the detective. In a rough and rugged voice, the officer responded, "We have not classified the disappearance of Thomas as a kidnapping. For now, he is simply a child who has gone missing. I believe your children will be safe. Now if you'll excuse me, I need to go and speak with Mr. and Mrs. Grant."

Sal was now mixed with emotions. On one hand he was pleased. He managed to squeeze out another piece of information he did not have—the name of the missing boy was Thomas. Thomas Grant. Sure, he could have gleaned this information from the neighbors, but he hadn't lost his touch. On the other hand, he was unsettled. Something in the eyes and demeanor of the detective didn't sit right with him.

Friday September 13th – 8:00 p.m
Grant Residence (735 Franklin Lane)

IN THE STUDY OFF to the right of the foyer and across the hall from the library, Detective Wilson sat and questioned Mr. and Mrs. Grant.

Mrs. Sylvia Grant, on the right side of forty, spent most of her days volunteering at school functions and local charities. She carried a slender yet well-proportioned frame that stood six feet tall. She wore a black princess-cut dress with a slit running up the left thigh accentuating her toned runners' legs. Jet black hair that fell to her shoulders was highlighted with the trailing sunlight parsing the window in the study. She accented the outfit with simple yet elegant white Akoya Cultured pearls that traced the long strokes of her neck.

Mr. Douglas Grant, on the opposite side of forty, held the honor of being the bread winner for the family. The CEO of Orbitz Technology, a software firm that specialized in virtual reality emulation rendering, he was seated to the right of his wife. Outfitted in a three-piece charcoal Windsor suit designed by Tom Ford, he had a slight twitch of the hands as Detective Wilson relayed his questions.

"So, let's go over this one more time," said Wilson.

"Damn it!" exclaimed Mr. Grant. "We have already told you the story twice, and you are sitting here doing nothing to find our son."

Mrs. Grant shed a silent tear.

"Mr. Grant," continued the detective. "I know how frustrating this is for you and your wife. We are doing everything we can to find your son. If you listen closely, you'll hear the hum of our police helicopter circling your community. They are coordinating with the team on the ground to scope out places of interest. We have another team following the different routes your son may have used to make this way home. In finding your son, we need to do our part, and you need to do your part. Your part Mr. Grant, is helping us to understand who may have wanted to take your son."

At those words, Mrs. Grant gave a shutter and another tear trickled down her cheek and caught at the tip of her chin.

"Fine!" uttered Mr. Grant. "Just find him. Find Tommy! Find our son."

"Thank you, sir. Now, please tell me the story again."

Agitated, Douglas Grant launched into the story.

"Earlier in the day, Tommy sent us a message asking if he could go to Josh's house to play basketball after school. We agreed he could do so, but he had to be home before six o'clock. Sylvia and I were to meet our board of directors at a dedication ceremony. My company, Orbitz Technology, dedicated $3 million to build and fund a technology campus on Martin Luther King Blvd. This campus was designed to teach children who are considered underprivileged about the world of technology and how the use of technology could forge a future for them and their families. I grew up in a household that didn't have much, and at times we had to scrape together to survive."

Wilson nodded his head to signify he was following along.

"Detective Wilson." Douglas fixed on him with his dark brown eyes. "Orbitz Technology was my dream since I was Tommy's age, and it was always something I wanted to pass along to my son."

Mrs. Grant slightly lowered her head.

"The name came from the idea that the sky is not the limit. There is so much more out there if only you can expand your mind beyond conventional thinking. Anyway," he sighed. "The dedication dinner was tonight at 8pm. A dinner we missed because of the tragedy – this nightmare, that has unfolded with our family as the starring actors."

Wilson noticed from his peripherals the constant, yet silent movements of Mrs. Grant asked. "Mr. Grant, being a man of substantial wealth, you're bound to generate your share of enemies. Many times, people believe your enemies come as a result of a slight or an argument, but that is not always the case. You can have an enemy who materializes simply because of who you are and what you stand for. Can you think of anyone that could fit into either one of those categories?"

"No. None. Not at all. I do not have any enemies I could think – no I don't have any."

Wilson recognized the shaky tone in his voice that had not been there before. "Mr. Grant, if there is something that you know or someone you suspect, the best thing you can do is to tell me everything. This is the most important way you can help at this point."

Defiantly, Douglas looked at the detective and said, "Rob, you've known Sylvia and me since we moved into this community. At the time Thomas, Tommy, was five years old. In those six years of community events, have you ever seen me cross words with anyone? Have you ever seen anyone have cross words with me? We are a tight community here, except for... well, no need to go there. When I tell you, I could not fathom who would take our son, take my word for it. I do not have a clue."

"I believe you, Doug. Please understand I have to ask these questions." Detective Wilson turned his attention to Mrs. Grant, "Sylvia."

At the mention of her name, that far away glaze Sylvia Grant had begun to exhibit seemed to shift to the features of Detective Rob Wilson's face.

"Do you know of anyone who may want to harm your son? Have there been any changes in his mood, routines, or activities? Is there anything you can think of that would aide in our search for Thomas?"

Moving her hand to the end table, Mrs. Grant slowly removed the bottle of water from the tabletop, pulled the bottle to her lips, and took a drink. A drink larger than a sip and less than a gulp. Satiated, she replaced the bottle on the end table and spoke.

"Rob, everything with Tommy has been as normal as can be. He has not mentioned any kind of bullying at school, his grades are as high as they have been, and I have not seen any strange people around. Well, none except for Donatella Bianchi. Douglas may not want to say it, but I know we are all thinking it. The fact we would let a woman like that in our neighborhood sours me to my core. No one put up a fight. No one! And now look what has happened. She has taken my son!"

Unfolding her left foot from behind her right ankle, Sylvia crossed her left leg over her right. The widening slit in her dress slowly crept its way up her thigh exposing her long limb enough that with just another half inch would probably expose things only meant for Douglas.

"You need to go and question that... that... child molester!" Sylvia spewed with venom in her words and hate in her eyes. "If she has had anything to do with the disappearance of my son, she will wish she had never been born."

"Sylvia!"

"Mrs. Grant!"

Both Douglas and Detective Wilson exclaimed at the same time.

"Don't deny it, hon. You know the thought has run through your mind. The math adds up. This is a gated community. One that we have lived in for over six years. And nothing, absolutely nothing like this has ever happened before. Yet this harlot who preys on little boys has lived here for only three months and this happens. Why the hell is she here anyway? And you men did not put up any fight of her moving in here because she's 'gorgeous'. Well damn it, that 'gorgeous' child-molesting bitch has now taken my son. My son! And I have to sit here and answer these fruitless questions. Go knock on her door, better yet, go kick in her door, and bring my son home to me!"

"Mrs. Grant, let's calm down. There is no proof of her involvement at this point in time. I assure you we are following every lead and she will certainly be questioned as well." In the back of his mind, Detective Wilson was already working an angle. When interviewing suspects, lexicon and body language become extremely crucial in breaking a case. A husband who talks about his missing wife in the past tense, typically signifies she has met some nefarious end and he knows to what end she has met.

Thus far in the interview with the Grant's, Mr. Grant intermingled his words in describing Tommy. Shifting between, "our son" and "my son." However, Mrs. Grant has only continued to use "my son." While not a smoking gun, another piece was gnawing at Detective Wilson. When Mr. Grant would mention "my son" or a reference to "his son," she began to fidget. Noticeably and yet almost unconsciously.

"Mrs. Grant, I have another question for you," said Detective Wilson.

Just then there was commotion coming from the foyer. One of the detectives, Detective Carl Ridder, walked into the study and approached Detective Wilson. He leaned down, whispered in his ear, and handed him a clear plastic evidence bag. Mr. and Mrs. Grant watched the exchange between the two detectives with looks that were a mixture of hope and anxiousness.

Steadying himself with a deep yet controlled breath, Detective Wilson held up the evidence bag and asked the Grants if they could identify this as the cell phone that belonged to their son.

The air left their lungs as they noticed the white customized phone case. It was a picture of Tommy, Douglas, and Sylvia. However, the case was no longer white, the case was now smeared with blood. Too much blood to be a simple cut.

3
FRIDAY, SEPTEMBER 13TH – 8:45 P.M
DRIFTWOOD SPRINGS NEIGHBORHOOD

The announcement broadcast over the walkie-talkie frequency chilled the search team to the core. The cell phone of Thomas Grant had been found and was positively identified by the boy's parents. While Tommy had been missing for nearly four hours, the search party secretly prayed he had just met up with another friend, lost track of time, and would turn up with no harm to his person. Unfortunately, they now knew this was not the case.

No other traces of Thomas had been found, and as the sunlight continued to dim into dusk the hope of finding additional clues had become tenuous. The search crew consisted of twenty of the Grants' friends and neighbors. The twenty had been split into five groups of four. Each group was then split into teams of two directed to walk through the subdivision on opposite sides of the street. They utilized this method in hopes of clearing a street with one pass and thus increasing the efficiency of their process.

The local police department deployed another twenty

officers from their SNR, Search and Rescue, team. This team came equipped with their own K-9 unit. This unit would start at the house belonging to the Grants to obtain a scent of Thomas. From there they would go to the neighbor's house where Thomas was last seen and begin their walking search, following closely behind their K-9 companion. The rescue team also deployed their Airbus H125 helicopter, better known as Harry. Harry, their eyes from the skies, utilized a SX-16 Nightsun searchlight that illuminated the area once the sun set.

Headed south down Foxhound Rd towards Kearny Way, the Thompson's caught up with the couple they were paired with in the sector they were to cover.

Yelling across the street above the whir of the helicopter's rotor blades, Marcellous asked, "Were you guys able to find any artifacts that could be useful in finding Tommy?"

The couple walked across the street to make their way toward the Thompson's. The man responded. "Unfortunately we haven't found anything. How about you guys?"

"Same here. We haven't found anything of note. By the way, my name is Marcellous Thompson and this is my wife Jasmyn," Marcellous said, outstretching his right hand.

Grasping the proffered hand and giving it a firm shake, the man responded, "Bill and Diane Dresser." Pointing to himself and then his wife with his left hand. "Nice to meet you, even under these dire circumstances. How long have you lived in the subdivision?"

"We moved into our home on Garden Street a little over four months ago," stated Jasmyn. "It's shocking to hear something like this could happen to a family so close to us. It's bad enough it happened, but –" Jasmyn shuddered.

Marcellous comforted his wife with a gentled touch to her shoulders and a kiss to her forehead.

Speaking for the first time since the foursome came together, Diane said, "This is absolutely awful. We have known the Grants for years and we've had them over to our house on several occasions. Poor Douglas and Sylvia. They must be devastated."

Making the left-hand turn onto Kearny Way, Diane continued, "I have a firm suspicion about who the cops should be looking at first."

"Diane, we shouldn't start spreading unfounded accusations," Bill chided his wife with a glance of displeasure.

"Bill, we never should have allowed 'Donatella the child molester' in our community. We had a pure feel to our neighborhood and her inclusion through the gate has been an unmitigated disaster that we now cannot undo."

Not sure yet of what to make of Diane and her comments, Marcellous thought to himself, *this neighborhood is not as "pure" as she would think*. Finding his voice, Marcellous stated, "We have yet to encounter Donatella. In fact, I think we've only seen her once and that was in passing as she drove through the gate as we entered."

With a wry smile, Bill said, "When you meet her in person, you will not be disappointed." Diane jabbed him in his left shoulder while raising an eyebrow.

Who is this woman that every man seems to be fawning over but at the same time elicits such disdain from the women? thought Marcellous.

"Where exactly does she live?" asked Jasmyn

"A timely question," hissed Diane. "Her lair is ahead on the left at the corner of Kearny Way and Calgary Lane. A perch with a view that allows her to spy over the community while waiting to dig her claws into more unsuspecting prey."

Bill rolled his eyes.

"We should pay special attention to her property as we close out our sector," continued Diane. "I don't trust that woman. I just know she had something to do with the disappearance, and I don't want to give her time to hide any evidence that could lead to the recovery of Thomas."

Approaching the aforementioned intersection, the quartet abandoned their grid style search pattern and cautiously approached the wrought iron fence surrounding Donatella's property. Hesitant in their decision-making process, Diane strolled up to the fence and pulled at the gate – locked. But she would not be deterred. Diane placed both hands at the top of the flat portion of the gate and with deft movement, propelled herself over the fence. Shocked at the forwardness of his wife, Bill scrambled and with the same type of agility cleared the fence in one fluid motion.

"Marcellous, this isn't right. We do not have the right to enter this person's private property. While many people suspect her of this evil deed, entering her property is something we need to leave up to the police."

As always, his wife was spot on with her assessment of the situation. "Babe, you're right. But I think when it comes to the safety of a child, there are a few rules that need to be bent."

"Bent!" Jasmyn exclaimed. "Really Marcellous!? So, if the roles were reversed, and we were the ones accused of this heinous crime, would you want the rules to be bent and for these neighbors to be traipsing all over our property?"

"Jasmyn, you know that's not what I mean. I just think..."

"What exactly is it you think, Marcellous?"

In their few years of marriage, Marcellous had not won an argument with her, and he knew this would not be the first one. Marcellous thought to himself, *of all women to defend this Donatella and her civil liberties, it has to be my wife.*

"I think we should, at most, go in and tell the Dresser's that this is a bad idea and that we should allow the police to deal with her."

"I'm not going over that fence, Marcellous!"

"Fine – I'll hop the fence, find the Dresser's, and pull them back." Leaning in to kiss his wife on the lips, she slightly turned her face, and he caught the corner of her mouth. *I'm going to be in the doghouse for this one.*

Attempting to lighten the mood as he headed for the fence, Marcellous said, "At least the separation of this fence keeps me even further away from Officer Lewis." Not waiting to hear Jasmyn's response, Marcellous took three long strides and with the quickness of a cheetah elevated and cleared the fence.

The first thing Marcellous could tell even in the pending darkness was the well-manicured lawn. *I need the name of her landscape company; this stuff is so plush and green.* The pathway was lit with Hampton Bay Low-Voltage Path Lights. *Looks like those run off of solar power. And is that a family of Gnomes? I'm beginning to like this woman more and more,* thought Marcellous.

Each gnome was inscribed with a saying. "Gnome is where the heart is," "Gnome sweet gnome," and "You don't gnome me." Marcellous couldn't help but chuckle as he finished reading the inscriptions. *Do what you came in here to do.*

Looking around the sprawling front yard, Marcellous spotted Diane and Bill. Not wanting to put this off any longer, Marcellous took off in a trot until he came face to face with the Dresser's.

"Guys," Marcellous interjected. "We should leave the search of her private property to the police. Think of it this way, if there is something that could incriminate her, we are officially ruining the evidence simply by being in here."

Acquiescing to his request, the three proceeded to the gate. When they arrived, they noticed Jasmyn with a panicked look on her face and once they surveyed the scene they knew why.

"Is there a reason you are trespassing on this property?" questioned the detective.

Looking at the name on his badge, Marcellous responded, "Detective Ridder, we were just finishing up our sector."

"As a civilian, you are not to enter private property. I need you to leave immediately."

The three with their hands caught in the cookie jar jumped one after the other back over the fence. First Marcellous, followed by Bill, and finally Diane joined the group back on the appropriate side of the fence.

"Your search has come to an end. You need to make your way back to your homes. We will handle the search from here."

Slipping away with their tails between their legs, Marcellous noticed that Detective Ridder was by himself. *Odd, I thought they were searching in pairs.*

Friday, September 13th – 9:20 p.m
Grant Residence (735 Franklin Lane)

Handing his wife the bottle of water that had caused condensation on the coffee table, Douglas' hands were visibly shaking. His eyes had become sunken and vacant as he pondered the news of the bloody cell phone.

Mrs. Grant wasn't in much better shape. The distant look that she exhibited earlier had returned but was paired with a hollow intensity that had overcome her features.

"Sylvia, Douglas, I have a few more questions that I need to ask." Looking firmly over at Mrs. Grant, Detective Wilson continued. "In law enforcement we utilize all available means of communication at our disposal to whittle down the truth."

Sylvia shifted.

"During our earlier interview, I couldn't help but notice some language and nonverbal communication of note."

The vacant look that had consumed Mrs. Grant had disappeared, and her eyes were now firmly focused on the detective.

"Sylvia, is there anything that you would like to share with me and probably your husband?"

Steely-eyed, Sylvia simply stated, "No, Rob, there isn't anything I want to share." With a sharpness in her tone.

"Well, Sylvia" Detective Wilson retorted, "I couldn't help but notice the way in which you mentioned your possessives of Thomas in contrast to the way in which Douglas did."

Sylvia's eyes narrowed.

"Is there a logical reason in which you could only refer to Thomas as 'my son' versus 'our son'?"

Douglas interjected, "Rob, it's likely just the stress of the situation."

"No doubt the situation is stressful, but I believe there is more to it than that. Ain't that right, Sylvia?"

"What are you saying?" questioned Douglas uncomprehendingly.

"Sylvia, let's lay all the cards on the table. It's no time to play games. Thomas's life is at stake. Is Douglas Thomas's father?"

"Rob!" exclaimed Douglas. "That is preposterous. Of course Thomas is my son. How dare you make such an unfounded accusation?"

"It's not as preposterous as you think, Douglas."

"Enough, damn it!" shouted Sylvia. "Enough. Honey, I'm sorry. I'm sorry."

"Sorry? What are you sorry for? Are you telling me, are you telling me that Thomas is not my son?"

"Douglas, you were gone all the time as you were starting your company, and I was always so lonely. So lonely." A tear materialized in the corner of her left eye. "One day, well, one night when you left for another work trip, I believe it was to Chicago, I decided to go to the local bar to grab a drink. I came across a guy who was charming, charismatic, and available at that moment. I fought it and told him that I was married. And though I was thinking, *no this isn't the right thing to do*, I secretly wanted him to ravish my body."

At that mention, Douglas looked as if he had thrown up in his mouth.

"He went on to tell me that he too was married, but on

that night he could be all mine. If I didn't tell, he wouldn't tell. Stomach twisting and turning. Mind flipping and calculating. Another lonely night at home on the docket for that evening, I dove in. Honey, I swear I felt horrible and would have taken it back if I could have. But I couldn't. I can't." Tears now streamed down her exquisite face.

With even, calm, and daggered eyes, Douglas asked, "Who is Thomas's father?"

"Honey, it doesn't matter at this po..."

"WHO IS HIS FATHER!"

Lowering her eyes and calculating the odds in front of her, Sylvia blurted out, "Bill."

"Bill who?"

"Douglas."

"Answer me, damn it!"

"Bill... Dresser."

"What the fuck, Sylvia! Bill Dresser! How in the hell did you sleep with Bill? We have only lived here for six years."

"Though I wanted Thomas to be your biological son, I always had an eerie feeling that it wasn't right. The math kept coming back to Bill. It took me a year to find him, and once I did, it took me another six months before I could muster the courage to approach him with my suspicions. Finally, I did. I told him. I told him that my son was probably his son. To my shock, he didn't push back. He agreed that he would be willing to take a paternity test. We scheduled the time, went to the appointment, and had to wait an agonizingly long three weeks for the DNA test to be returned. The results confirmed the worst... well, at least the worst for me. Later I found out that Diane could not have children and for Bill this was an opportunity to have a kid that he always wanted. He suggested he would keep the secret safe, but he also wanted to see his son. He told me that..."

"Is that why you pressured me to move into this community? Sylvia, that is sick! You are sick. You fucking bitch! I could..."

"Douglas honey, I'm sorry. I'm so sorry."

"You're sorry. That's all you can say to me? Sorry. I raised Thomas as if he was my son. I stayed up with him when he was sick. Took him to the doctor when he broke his arm. I started making plans for him to be the heir of my company. My company. The dream I have had since I was a young boy. You selfish, selfish..."

Sylvia moved closer to her husband.

"Don't you dare put your filthy hands on me. Don't touch me!" Douglas stood up and started pacing the room. "The bonding time we spent playing conquer the mountain and making forts while inside the house. The time we spent at my parents' house. My parents only grandchild is not their grandchild. Your lies and deceit are ruining lives, Sylvia."

Stunned into silence, Sylvia found her footing yet again.

"This doesn't change the fact that our son is missing," Sylvia said, recovering.

"Oh... now it's our son!" Douglas spit on the ground. "Maybe his father kidnapped him. That's who needs to be investigated." Struggling to master his emotions with his heart pounding audibly through his rib cage and blood rushing to his ears, Douglas collapsed to the ground.

Noticing her husband now prostate on the ground and thinking to herself, *maybe it's better if he died. I do have the insurance policy*. She did her wifely duties and rushed to his side.

Immediately regaining his wits and yanking his arm from the grasp of his wife, Douglas spewed, "I told you don't put your filthy hands on me!" Accepting aide from Rob who had become the forgotten man in this drama, Douglas was moved to the chair opposite to his wife.

"You know, Sylvia," Douglas said coldly between drinks of water, "secrets can flow in both directions and can cut as deadly as a guillotine."

Not sure how to respond, she raised her eyebrow.

"Yeah my dear, Sylvia, I'm not so sure my secret can come close to topping the bombshell you just laid, but it is something I have wanted to share for a while."

Shock registering on her face, Sylvia's heart rhythms became abnormal.

"You remember Shana, your gay twin sister who has been virtually disowned by the family. Well as it turns out, she is not gay. Not at all. In reality, she is bi. And babe, she hungers for entry through the back door. And for me, that back door is always unlocked! I guess it kind of runs in the family. You spread your legs, she spreads her ass. Face it, hon, you're a prude. You have no sense of adventure between the sheets, whereas Shana had no inhibitions. From being cuffed to the headboard to erotic asphyxiations, she never batted an eye, just always willing to please. Matter of fact, she pleased me several times in the very chair your ass is adorning at this moment."

Unable to hold in her emotions and as quick as sound, Sylvia rushed Douglas. Before Rob could catch hold of her, she lunged at her husband with all of her body weight and toppled the chair over backwards.

Pelting his face and with the wail of a banshee, she struck him. "You sorry sack of shit!"

Breathing heavily, Sylvia was extracted from her bleeding husband by Detective Wilson. Flailing and out of control, the moment was once again broken with the entrance of Detective Ridder.

Lightly dumping Mrs. Grant into a chair and making his way back to assist Mr. Grant, Detective Wilson implored Ridder to speak.

"Well, sir. We've found some clothes on the property of Donatella Bianchi that we believe belong to Tommy. Sir, they are covered in blood."

SATURDAY, SEPTEMBER 14TH – 7:00 AM
DETECTIVE WILSON RESIDENCE (407 PARK LANE)

Headline: *Missing Child in NC Suburbs*
www.TheSalReport.com
By: Sal Grandson

On Friday evening, September 13th, around 5:00 p.m in the Driftwood Springs community, an eleven-year-old boy, Thomas Grant, disappeared on his way home from a friend's house. Law enforcement along with concerned citizens within the community canvased the area well into the fall of darkness, but there has been no concrete clues to Thomas's whereabouts. Sources close to the case stated there are two pieces of evidence the detectives are following up on as of this publication. The first, a cell phone covered in blood has been shared with the Grants, and they have identified this as the phone that belonged to their son. At this time, the blood is not confirmed to be that of Thomas Grant, though nonetheless the phone has been taken to the lab for further analysis.

The second and most intriguing is a set of clothes authorities suspect belongs to Thomas Grant. Again, this has not been confirmed and additional test will be run. The location in which the clothing was found has not been disclosed, but my sources say they may point to a suspect in the case.

Neighbors have set up a vigil at the home of the Grants and plan to continue their search at first light. God speed to the search team, and I pray for the safe return of Thomas Grant.

DETECTIVE WILSON FUMED as he read this information. A freelance journalist by the name of Sal Grandson had information about the case that had not been shared with any media outlet. Yet, Grandson knew more than he should and more than Wilson was prepared to share with the media at this time. Now that the story had been shared and appeared to be picked up by several local news stations, he would need to control the story. For now, he needed to focus on other elements of the case. He made a mental note to find out more about this Sal Grandson, and he also needed to know where he was obtaining his information.

Monday, September 16th – 7:00 p.m
Donatella's Residence (300 Calgary Lane)

AT THE CORNER of Kearny Way and Calgary Lane, a two-story Signature Chateau loomed. The exterior of the home consisted of two walkout balconies that framed the corners of the house. The balcony on the left extended to the forefront of the structure while the one on the right was set to the background. The house itself was made of natural stone that tinged tannish gray from the illumination of the moonlight. Its windows and the doorway both arched skyward with white trim. The house sat quietly as if it slumbered through the night.

Walking through the perfectly manicured lawn were detectives Wilson and Ridder. Apprehensive of what they could encounter, both Wilson and Ridder stalked cautiously with their right hands hovering over the butts of their police issued Sig Sauer P226 semiautomatic handgun. Wilson rang the doorbell while Ridder shifted his eyes from one window to another, looking for any sign of movement. With a second ring of the doorbell, the sound of light footfalls on what sounded like solid marble flooring hit their ears. Ten seconds later, the electronic deadbolt lock disengaged from the reinforced door jamb. The door swung open and in that instant time momentarily stopped.

There stood a wondrous specimen with piercing hazelnut brown eyes. A smooth golden-brown complexion with jet black curly hair that rested seductively on her shoulders. She wore large platinum hoop earrings that shimmered when kissed by the chandelier light hung within the foyer. Before speaking, she ran her tongue right to left over the nude lip gloss that accentuated her doughy upper lip.

In an assertive, feminine, Southern drawl Donatella Bianchi asked, "Detectives, how may I help you?" She ran her hand through her silky hair and eyed each officer in turn suspiciously.

Wilson composed himself from the carnal lust-filled thoughts that now pushed for space in the forefront of his mind. "Ms. Bianchi," Wilson stammered. "We have a few questions we need to ask you in connection to the disappearance of Thomas Grant."

"Yes, Thomas Grant. I heard he had gone missing earlier, doubtless with my past, you'd consider me a suspect. Isn't that right detective? No need to answer."

Donatella raised her hand, cutting off Wilson's words before they could escape his lips. "The thought is written all over your face, and by the way your junior lackey is poised to pounce, I'd say you didn't just come for a social chat."

"Well Ms. Bianchi, do you mind if we come in for a few moments to go over a few questions?" Recovered Wilson.

Knowing she couldn't resist the inquires of the officers without adding more suspicion than necessary and potentially bringing more prying eyes into her home than she wanted, Donatella said, "Sure, come on in, officers."

As Donatella began to lead the detectives from the front door through the foyer, Wilson obtained a full view of her incredible figure. A curvy yet athletic build with a graceful stride, as if she were walking down the runway in Paris. He thought to himself, *a photo shopped image could not piece together a more perfect woman as well as nature and her mother had done.*

Passing by the dual curved staircases in the foyer that lead to the second floor, they entered what appeared to be the living room. A 65-inch Sony flat screen TV hung over a wood burning fireplace that looked as if it has been burning for a few hours from the amount of ash that had accumulated.

"Make yourselves comfortable," Donatella stated as she lowered herself onto the leather sofa that sat in the center of the spacious room. "What can I do for you this evening?"

"Where were you Friday evening between the hours of 3:00 p.m and 7:00 p.m?" asked Detective Wilson.

"Look!" Donatella stated with a note of irritation in her voice. "We can spend the next thirty minutes to an hour engaging in this fruitless questioning and getting absolutely nowhere, or you can simply tell me why you are here so I can get back to my evening."

"Ms. Bianchi, you do not dictate the manner in which we conduct our questioning!" blasted Ridder, speaking for the first time.

"Listen Detective Ridder," she said, glancing down to his badge. "You are a guest in my home. And the last time I checked I'm under no formal obligation to answer any of your questions. So, either you get to the point, or you get out my home."

Ridder, turning a slight shade of pink from the blood pulsating under his skin retorted, "You listen –"

Wilson slowed his younger colleague with a hand gesture. "We found some bloody clothes that appear to be the last outfit Thomas Grant was seen in on the day of his disappearance. That outfit was found buried in your front yard."

With a raised eyebrow and a questioning look, Donatella spoke, "Oh really, and where in my front yard was a set of incriminating articles discovered?"

"In the dirt between your three gnomes and flower bed," sneered Detective Ridder. "So again, where were you and what were you doing?"

Considering her options fully and knowing any alibi she gave could not be validated Donatella Bianchi simply stated, "I'd like to call my lawyer."

"In that case," stated Detective Wilson. "We are

formally placing you under arrest in the disappearance of Thomas Grant. You have the right to remain silent..." Wilson droned.

Donatella, thinking quickly, stated, "I'd like to make my phone call prior to leaving my home."

"No! You can have your phone call at the station, you sick twisted pervert. You may have gotten away with this before, but I guarantee we will throw the book at you," said Detective Ridder. Smelling of old tobacco and cheap beer, he maneuvered closer to her ear and whispered, "You are gonna burn, you sadistic bitch!"

Tuesday, September 17th – 7:30 a.m
Police HQ (One Police Plaza)

"Ms. BIANCHI, your story doesn't add up to me. We will sit here all morning until you are begging to tell me the truth," stated Detective Wilson.

"Damn it, detective. I have been answering your questions for hours and I have yet to have my one call. I demand a phone now, or your entire department will be brought up on charges," Donatella said in a curt voice.

"With all due respect, you do not have a leg to stand on. We have you dead to rights. You're better off confessing to Thomas's abduction. If you tell us where he is right now, we will ensure the DA takes your cooperation into consideration."

Donatella cut Wilson a glare with her hazelnut brown eyes, which caused him to shutter as a cold chill ran down the base of his spine.

Leaning forward in her seat, tucking the curls behind her left ear and with even menace in the tone of her voice, Donatella said, "Detective, this is the last time I'm going to say this, and I want you to hear me clearly. Get your ass out of that chair, open the door that is situated behind you, walk down that hallway, and bring me back a phone. There is more at stake than your feeble mind can understand."

"I wish I could, but I need you to help me understand something first, Donatella. I can call you Donatella, right? Help me understand what is so dire and what is at play that I do not understand. If Thomas Grant is in some danger because of where you have stored him, I implore you to tell me where he is so that we can save him. At this point the only charge against you is kidnapping a minor. Sure, you have a prior conviction and sentencing could be a tad tricky, but if he should die I can guarantee your pretty little ass will never see daylight again."

"Detective, Thomas Grant is the least of my concerns. I had nothing to do with his disappearance. In fact, his safety or lack thereof is a matter of your inability to do your job. You are wasting your time and you are wasting my time."

A blue light above Donatella's head began to blink. Annoyed at the interruption, Detective Wilson sighed and stated, "I'll be back shortly. Make yourself comfortable. You're going to be here until we have a full confession."

Wilson slid back his metal chair, scraping the concrete floor, and walked judiciously out of interview room number three. Looking for the source of the interruption, Wilson found Officer Johnson.

"This had better be important, Johnson!"

"Sir, we have two problems, and I rushed here to give you the latest. Around 7:00 this morning it was determined that one of the kids in the Driftwood Springs subdivision had not checked in at school. When the absentee notice was sent to the parents, they called the school to say that their daughter had left at her normal time. Frantically, the mother has called our office in light of what happened with the other kid, Thomas Grant."

"Damn it!" uttered Wilson. "Maybe Bianchi has an accomplice. This would explain why Thomas Grant had not been found on the grounds of her residence. We need to turn up the heat on this woman. She is certainly hiding something, and we need to get to the bottom of it if we expect to see either one of these kids returned to their parents safely."

"Sir, that's the other point I need to make. The woman we have in interview room number three. Her name is not Donatella Bianchi."

"What?" exclaimed Wilson.

"Sir, it actually gets worst. Not only is her name not Donatella Bianchi, she has never been convicted as a child molester."

Stunned into silence, Wilson asked, "Johnson, what in the hell are you talking about?"

"Sir, her real name is Donatella Dabria, and she works for the FBI. The woman we have in custody is Special Agent Donatella Dabria. The call came in for the Charlotte field office. They have demanded her immediate release."

"Holy shit! Are you sure about this, Johnson?"

"Yes, sir. The FBI stated they are sending a team, and they expect to have Agent Dabria freed before they arrive. They will be here in five minutes."

Wilson couldn't believe what he had just heard, and with his head still reeling he was unsure of his next course of action. He knew pinning this abduction on Bianchi, or whatever the hell her name was, had the ring of truth to it. Now he was being told that his prime suspect needed to be released.

"Sir."

"Damn it, Johnson! Stop calling me sir."

"Yes, sir. Sorry sir... Sorry. Detective Wilson, what are we going to do?"

Leaving the young detective in his wake, Wilson walked back into interview room three. "Who in the hell are you?"

"Ahh," said Special Agent Dabria in her silky-smooth voice. "Looks like you have been contacted by my employers. I suggest you remove these handcuffs and return my belongings as I'm sure my ride will be here within ten minutes."

"Less than five actually," said Wilson under his breath.

"Well, looks like we do not have time to waste. Move with all due haste detective. I would hate to keep more members of the FBI waiting, as I have waited for my one phone call all night long."

"Special Agent Dabria, let me apologize for the manner in which you were treated. I had just left the room to obtain a phone for you when I was given the news."

"I see, Detective Wilson. You were just heading out to bring me a phone. If I had to guess, I would say that blue light that is stationed roughly seven feet above my seated position began to blink. It informed you of a more pressing matter that required your immediate attention, other than affording me due process of the law. How am I doing so far? No need, because I'm sure what happened next is you were informed that you had made a gross mischaracterization about one Ms. Donatella Bianchi. Of course, we had our reason for the deception, one in which I'm not at liberty to discuss with you at this moment. What I am interested in is why it took you three minutes to return, when in reality the news of my position with the FBI should have only taken a minute at most to discuss? Could it be that Thomas Grant has been found alive and well?"

"No, Thomas has not been found. In fact, the matter has been compounded. Another child in the subdivision has been abducted."

The intensity in SA Dabria's gaze sent another chill down the spine of Detective Wilson. "What is the name of the child who has been abducted?"

"I'm sorry. This is still within the local jurisdiction. I'm not at liberty to discuss an ongoing investigation."

"Is the name of the missing child Bree Singleton?"

"Yes, how did you –"

Standing quickly from her chair and striding to the interview room door, Donatella called back, "If there is one hair harmed on the head of that girl, I promise you will pay dearly by my own hands."

With that Donatella Dabria turned the handle of the heavy metal door, flung it open, and disappeared through the cleared doorway. That left Detective Wilson to wonder what he had just stepped into the middle of, and the vision of Donatella seared his memory.

Tuesday, September 17th – 5:30 a.m
Grandson Residence (4208 Jasper Road)

SAL GRANDSON, a creature of habit, had not broken one of the habits he learned during his time at the Daily, waking up extremely early in the morning. For nearly two decades Sal would wake up at 4:00 a.m to jog five miles on his treadmill, drink his cup of coffee, and plot a strategy for the day. And this morning, like many other mornings in his past, Sal did just that. With his workout behind him, he was now settling in for his cup of Joe and powering up his laptop to outline his day. At the top of his agenda was conducting some research on the Grant family. He had not been able to obtain much information after his article on Saturday, but the case was indeed still open. Before Sal dove into the paths he would take for his research into the Grants, he fired up his email client and quickly skimmed the subject lines for anything that was of interest. Three quarters of the way down the page, there was an email that immediately grabbed his attention.

Subject: Potential Suspect in Grant Disappearance at Police HQ

Priority: Urgent

From: Anonymous

A brief hesitation came over Sal as he was prepared to open the email. *What if this is a virus?* he thought. Sal had lost a computer to a virus before and as a result, he made daily backups of his computer in case the worst should happen again. Figuring he was a safe as he could be and curiosity getting the best of him, he finally opened the email.

The body of the email was short but held two pieces of vital information. The first piece of information stated the police had taken Donatella Bianchi into custody, and she would probably be released within a few hours. The second piece of information mentioned another child from the same neighborhood was now missing.

Sal had to read the email again to ensure he comprehended it correctly. So many questions were now going through his head. Would they need to release Donatella because the other disappearance took place while she was in custody? Who exactly was this Donatella Bianchi, and what role did she play in this case? Could Driftwood Springs be dealing with their own in community serial kidnapper, if this was indeed a kidnapping? Who was the second victim, and what was the connection, if any, to Thomas Grant? Though the questions were racing through his mind, he realized he had one more pressing question that needed to be answered.

"Who sent me this email?"

Two hours later, Sal found himself sitting in his beat-up 2002 Honda Accord. Though it had over 260,000 miles, it still purred like a kitten. He wasn't sure if sitting here would result in any additional details. Yes, the email said the suspect would likely be released today, but that didn't mean it was true. Furthermore, he didn't know if anything he read in that email was accurate. But deep in his gut Sal knew it was. He knew there had been an arrest, if one could call it that, and he knew there had been another abduction. He just needed to confirm this information prior to publishing any of it. While waiting outside of Police HQ, he shifted his research focus to that of Ms. Donatella Bianchi. What he found about the woman wasn't much, but nonetheless the tidbits he was able to pull together were juicy. Donatella had been convicted of child molestation, and there was a suit filed by the community that they did not want her living in Driftwood Springs. Looking through public information on the County Clerk's website, he saw the suit was accompanied by a petition signed by fifteen people in the community. He casually noticed the petition was signed by all women. Other than that, there wasn't much information about her. Sal couldn't help but think to himself how odd that was. Living in the digital age as we do, one can typically tell a great deal about a person by the digital footprint they leave. He considered himself to be a pretty private person, but his name carried all kinds of information about his time working for the New York Daily News. So, for this to be the only information about her on the web was strange. Strange indeed.

Suddenly, he noticed two black Chevy Tahoes with tinted windows pulling up to the police headquarters. He knew for a fact these were not police-issued vehicles, so he began to ponder who the vehicles belonged to and what they were doing here. Three seconds later the passenger door of the lead vehicle opened, and he noticed with amazement that this was the FBI. And not five seconds after that, the front door of the police department opened and a beautiful woman came striding with purpose from the door to the vehicle where the agent was still holding the front passenger door open. Once the woman stepped into the vehicle, the door shut, the agent moved to the rear of the vehicle, opened that door, and stepped into the truck. Once its door shut, the lead vehicle, followed by the second vehicle, pulled off.

Sal's head was spinning. What was going on here? Was that Donatella? If it was, why was she now in an FBI vehicle? One for which she was given the front seat and without any restraints. Something told him to get out of his car right now and head over to the police station. Never one to fight against his intuition, Sal hustled out of his vehicle and began rushing over to the building. Eyeballing the cross traffic, he saw there was an opening coming soon, but he would need to run to make it without incident. When the moment arose, Sal took off in a dead sprint crossing one lane, two lanes, three lanes, and finally four lanes of traffic. This last lane earned him a press of the horn by the vehicle passing by. *A little close, Sal buddy,* he thought, pulling down his button-up Kenneth Cole Reaction shirt. With the shirt back in place, he continued on his path to the door of the police station when the door opened.

Exiting from the front door was the detective in charge of the Thomas Grant case. In stride, Sal removed the Mead notebook from his back pocket and a well-chewed pen from the pocket of his shirt.

"Detective Wilson was that Donatella Bianchi that just left the station, and if it was, why was she getting into an FBI vehicle? Is she a suspect in the disappearance of Thomas Grant? Has there been any additional news of his disappearance?" Sal said all of this without taking a breath, hoping that something would spark a fire under the detective and get him talking. With that he finally said, "And what's this I hear about another kidnapping victim?"

Bingo! Sal thought as all forward motion of Detective Wilson ceased, and he turned to look at Sal.

"What did you say?" he asked in a gruff, raspy voice.

I said a lot, Sal quickly ran through his head, but he knew exactly what the detective was asking. "I said I heard there has been another victim. Can you confirm this is true?"

Detective Wilson measured him with those hard, detective's eyes, "Who are you and where exactly did you hear this information?"

"Salvatore Grandson, but everyone calls me Sal. And as to where I heard about this other victim, I cannot reveal my source." In truth Sal had no clue where this information had come from, and he certainly wasn't going to tell the detective he received it via email from someone he didn't know. "So, can you confirm this second victim?"

Wilson quickly retorted, "We do not comment on open and ongoing investigations."

"So, what you're saying is there has been a second victim and the cases are connected. Do we know how they are connected?"

"I never said there was a second victim and I certainly didn't say the two cases are connected."

"Great, so there are two cases." Sal said writing in his notebook. "You'll certainly let the public know if the two cases are connected in any way, right Officer?"

Looking haggard, feeling exasperated, and against his better judgement, Wilson responded, "Yes, there has been another disappearance, and at this time we are treating them as two separate cases. We are headed to speak with the family and better determine what has happened. That's all I can say for now." With that he slouched down into the cruiser, turned the engine over, and pulled away from the police headquarters.

5

TUESDAY, SEPTEMBER 17TH – 8:15 A.M
DONATELLA'S RESIDENCE (300 CALGARY LANE)

Donatella Dabria, the only daughter of an Italian mother and a Black American father, had lived her life for redemption and revenge. At the age of thirteen, Donatella's parents were eradicated by an entity calling themselves "The Syndicate." Her parents, murdered while overseas on a business trip for her father, never had the opportunity to see their daughter blossom. The news was given to her by her aunt, who had agreed to look after young Donatella while the couple had gone on the trip. Though it's still unknown if the explosion on the boat was meant for her father or the owner of their security firm, it never mattered to Donatella. The fact of the matter is they had killed her parents and for that they would pay.

Donatella vowed she would prepare both her mind and her body for the task ahead. Young in age and lacking in strength, Donatella began her training in Aikido. This Japanese martial art allowed the practitioner to utilize the momentum of their attacker into a variety of throws or joint locks. To expound on her techniques, Donatella then picked up Judo, another Japanese martial art that in addition to throws and joint locks helped to expand her methods of subduing her attacker. Understanding that many opponents she would face in the future would likely be armed, Donatella next turned her focus to Jiu-Jitsu. By the time she was eighteen and preparing to head off for college, Donatella could dispatch any attacker during the weekly sparing match with next to no effort.

However, Donatella was not solely focused on defense. She would need to go on the offense as well. For that Donatella moved to Krav Maga. A hand-to-hand combat discipline that focuses on brutal counter attacks as well as incapacitating her enemy by any means necessary. To master this last discipline, Donatella would need to increase her strength so in between college classes Donatella would strength train and push her cardio regimen. When it came to close quarters combat, no one, man or woman was better than Donatella Dabria. No one!

Understanding all combat would not be hand to hand and that as the saying went, one should not bring a knife to a gun fight, Donatella would need armed combat training. And of course, in order to put her hands on the members of The Syndicate, she would need a job that provided unfettered access to the best tracking technology. To achieve both objectives Donatella would work her way into the awaiting graces of the FBI. Armed combat did not come as naturally as hand-to-hand combat for Donatella, and for the first time in her life she was not first in class. In fact, through the first half of her training at the FBI academy her performance was considered subpar. As with everything else in her life, Donatella dug in her heels and pushed. She thought about her mother's last breath, and she pushed.

She thought about how her father would not give her away at her wedding, and she pushed. She thought about seeing every single one of those bastards pay for robbing her of her parents, then she pushed. She pushed her way to finish second in her class, and she pushed herself one step closer to achieving the goal she had coveted since she was thirteen.

Nonetheless, Donatella still had her day job to do, and this day job had just taken a drastic turn. A turn that would likely provide an opportunity for Donatella Dabria to unleash the skills she had spent a lifetime crafting.

Tuesday, September 17th – 8:30 a.m
Singleton Residence (315 Calgary Lane)

FRUSTRATED by the events of the previous night and ultimately mad at herself, Special Agent Dabria arrived at the home of Frank and Elizabeth Singleton. Formulating a plan of attack as she approached the subdued residence, she couldn't help but feel responsible for the disappearance of their only child, Bree. Her only job was to look after the well-being of this family, and she ended up being detained by the local police department for a crime she was neither interested in nor concerned about – until now. Some sick miscreant had kidnapped this young girl, a girl she swore to protect, and she planned to do everything necessary to bring her back home. She arrived at the ornate wooden door with diamond-shaped glass inlays and knocked three times on the solid structure.

Frazzled with bloodshot eyes that conveyed hours of

crying and a look that was both ghostly and distant, Mrs. Singleton stood with the door slightly ajar with a look of confusion mixed with anger as she stared at Agent Dabria. As she eyed the agent, her mind pondered whether to let her in or leave her there. Out there where she could think about how she let Bree down after she swore she would protect her with her last breath. Out there where she should be looking for their daughter instead of in the house asking questions. Out there because Elizabeth wasn't sure she wanted SA Dabria in her house.

"Mrs. Singleton," Agent Dabria stated, breaking the ice. "I'm sorry about Bree. I swear I will get her back. Let's go inside so we can talk, and I can formulate a plan to move forward."

Hesitantly and almost on autopilot, Elizabeth Singleton opened the door and ushered SA Dabria into her home. Finding her voice, she meekly stated, "Frank is in the family room," as the two awkwardly stood next to each other.

Without any additional conversation, Agent Dabria began her trek toward the family room as she pondered the reason for the kidnappings taking place in this community. It certainly didn't make any sense. This was by all accounts a quiet, nondescript part of town and not only had one event shaken the community but a second within a week. Mulling over the puzzle pieces that were disjointed within her mind, her gut continued to tell her that something was not right. Something was not adding up, and she now needed to figure out why.

"Donatella," the voice of Frank Singleton said, startling her out of her trance. "Thank you for stopping by."

"Frank, Elizabeth, tell me everything you know."

Driftwood Springs

"As with every day," started Frank, "we had breakfast, the three of us, in the kitchen at the island. Liz reviewed Bree's math homework as I put away the dishes and knotted my tie. Nothing seemed out of the ordinary, and Bree grabbed her book bag, lunch box, and blue windbreaker. She walked out of the door for the bus, and I continued my preparations for work. Shortly thereafter I made my way to the office. It wasn't until I received the frantic call from Liz that I began to worry."

"I tried you several times!" blurted Elizabeth angrily. "You were nowhere to be found! We trusted you, Donatella. Our entire family trusted you, and now – "

Before finishing her sentence, Elizabeth Singleton broke down into a full crying fit yet again. Frank held his wife, gently stroked her hair, and looked at Donatella, lost and directionless.

With a cold, calculating voice and eyes focused on Frank Singleton, Special Agent Dabria stated, "I will find who took Bree. I will bring her home safely. I promise you, they will never have the opportunity to hurt another child again!"

Frank could feel the conviction and truthfulness behind each word that she spoke. While still stroking the hair of his sobbing wife, Frank gave a barely perceptible nod to the only person he knew they could truly trust.

The sound of the doorbell interrupted the moment, and without prompting Donatella went to the door. As she made her way through the foyer, she could tell through the glass windowpanes within the door the all-too-familiar blue Caprice Classic used by detectives that had not yet moved into the 20th century.

"Detective Wilson, what a pleasant surprise."

"Special Agent Dabria, what are you doing here?"

"If you haven't heard, Detective Wilson, there is another child missing from this fine community, with very little positive progress being made by the police department. I took it upon myself to inform the Singleton's that I'll take a personal interest in the recovery of their daughter."

"You have no right to insert yourself into an active investigation. The FBI has no jurisdiction, and I have not invited you into this case."

"Yes, jurisdiction you say. Well, when the police department has shown an utter and complete lack of competency, especially when the welfare of a child is at stake, I do not wait for an invitation, and I surely do not wait for jurisdiction. Would you like to waltz into the family room and alert Mr. and Mrs. Singleton that you have refused my help because of that burdensome and truthfully archaic rule. While you're at it, you can let them know that you purposelessly held me all night in the disappearance of Thomas Grant only to release me. I'm sure that will give them all the confidence they need that you and your jurisdiction will find their only child."

Fuming internally and trying not to show the steam building under his collar, Detective Wilson said, "You can sit in on the interview, but I'm running the show."

"No need," SA Dabria said. "I have a more pressing engagement and have already asked all the questions I need at this time. Do keep me apprised if you stumble across anything of value."

With a slight nod of courtesy, Agent Donatella Dabria exited the Singleton's residence, walked down the path leading away from the house, and entered her home directly across the street.

TUESDAY, SEPTEMBER 17TH – 9:00 A.M
UNDISCLOSED LOCATION

"I trust you have everything under control and things are progressing as planned?" asked the mellow yet assertive voice from the other end of the phone.

"Yes indeed. We have successfully navigated the first phase of the plan, and everything fell into place exactly as you thought it would."

"And the FBI woman, Dabria. Has she started to suspect anything out of the ordinary?"

"Nothing yet. If I sense she is making substantial progress with her investigation of the children's disappearances, I'll execute the auxiliary portion of our plan. Until then, I will move on to the next phase of our plan within the next few hours."

"Excellent. Understand this part of the plan will carry the most risk you have experienced up to this point. Take all precautions to ensure you are not discovered. As it stands now, no one knows of our connection and no one can ever know of our connection. If for some reason you are discovered, my name and involvement cannot be uttered for any reason. Are we clear on this?"

"We're clear."

"Good. Keep me posted on your progress and remember what's at stake."

"I haven't forgotten. You do not need to remind me."

Tuesday, September 17th – 9:00 a.m
Donatella's Residence (300 Calgary Lane)

A<small>SCENDING</small> the helix style staircase of her chateau, Special Agent Dabria decided it was time she stepped out of her role and fully entrenched herself in the disappearances of Thomas Grant and Bree Singleton. In order to investigate the disappearances appropriately, she needed to shed the cover story of Donatella Bianchi, the convicted child molester, and officially introduce the patrons of Driftwood Springs to Donatella Dabria, the decorated Special Agent of the Federal Bureau of Investigations. The cover story worked to her advantage. Though she still received the gawking looks of the men, married and single, and the occasional woman, again married and single, within the subdivision, by and large she was left alone. No one visited her home for social calls, because they didn't want to be the pariah of the neighborhood for consorting with a known sex offender. This gave her the ability to hide in plain sight while conducting the surveillance necessary to accomplish her mission.

Accelerating through her bedroom into the spacious

walk-in closet, Donatella made her way to the safe hidden by the false panel that sat behind the 4x20 rows of shoes.

Throughout her career, Dabria found that working alone increased her probability of successful outcomes versus those in which a partner had been forced upon her. For some unknown reason, anytime she worked with a partner, some unfortunate event befouled them. Her first partner out the of academy, Terri Buckley, was hit by a ricocheting bullet in the ass while investigating their first case. With the injury being nothing more than a flesh wound, the doctors assured the agent the recovery would go fairly fast. Living for the moment of that first investigation and having to leave the investigation early via EMS, Buckley felt she had been cheated. Now she was champing at the bit to continue her normal duties. She pleaded day in and day out with her superior to move her back into the field early. She felt fine and knew she could be an asset to the organization. However, the agent in charge would not consider her fit for duty until the doctor had deemed her healthy. And that authorization would not come for at least a couple of weeks.

After two weeks on desk duty, SA Buckley pressed both the doctor and her superior until, they signed off on her fit-for-duty forms. It was mainly to get her out of their hair, so they could continue to do their jobs. Regardless of how she got there, Buckley was thrilled she was able to resume field work.

Again, being paired with SA Dabria, she was would be out on her second investigation. For SA Dabria, this would be her 4th. Each agent had been given a partner out of the academy, and with her partner going down the first week on the job, SA Dabria had been left to conduct a few investigations by herself, with the backing of the home office.

The first three saw nothing but success and began to get her noticed as an agent who produced results. Buckley knew she could produce as well and was excited to be back in the saddle. However, this excitement was tempered within the first hour they were on the streets.

Following up on a lead that a known weapons smuggler was held up in an apartment complex in the center of the city, agents Dabria and Buckley were dispatched to apprehend the assailant. Somehow, he must have been tipped off, because he was making his way up the fire escape when agents Dabria and Buckley came pounding on the door. Hearing the shuffling inside and what sounded like the movement of a window, the two forced their way into the apartment just in time to see their prey making his way up the fire escape.

Both agents quickly cleared the two-bedroom apartment before giving chase. Agent Buckley, eager to make her mark, was out of the window first. She scrambled up the metal steps with Agent Dabria following close behind. Though they took twenty seconds to clear the apartment before moving to the fire escape, the two were gaining ground quickly on the man they were sent to detain. He cleared the precipice of the roof, but Buckley was right on his six. The man running across the roof at top speed had nowhere to go.

In her gut Donatella felt something was not right about this chase. When they started, they were on the third floor. It would have been much simpler for the man to go down the two flights versus climbing the seven flights to a roof that seemingly went nowhere. As she began to give chase on the roof, Donatella noticed the peculiar route the man was taking while still racing at top speed. He wasn't running in a straight line and there were no obstacles in his path. With the route he was taking, Agent Buckley was closing on him even faster. All of a sudden it hit Donatella. Before she could warn her partner of the impending danger, she disappeared out of sight. Horrified about what she would find, Donatella cautiously made her way across the roof. When Agent Dabria arrived at the location where she saw her partner disappear, her fears were realized.

Their target knew someone would come looking for him at some point and as such had an escape route planned. At various locations on the roof there were man-sized holes that were covered with materials a slightly different color than that of the rest of the roof. Buckley, unaware of the trap, barreled ahead intent on capturing her man. Unsuspecting in her pursuit, she fell right through the roof.

Agent Buckley fell three stories onto a concrete slab, and by the time Agent Dabria had reached the hole she could tell Buckley had broken a leg, maybe both, had been knocked out, but was still alive. The pursuit could not continue. Dabria called in the situation as she reversed course to go and tend to her fallen partner.

When she arrived at the side of her partner, Dabria tried to revive Buckley while waiting for backup and the ambulance. After a few minutes, Buckley was awake but not yet aware of what happened. Donatella relayed the facts that led up to her current predicament in an effort to keep Buckley's mind off of the shear pain that had to be coursing its way through her body. Ironically enough Buckley had a moment of levity in her moment of extreme discomfort.

"You know," she grunted through clinched teeth. "Your

name... ahhh... your name is at odds with itself? Your first name," she grunted again "Donatella, means a Gift from God, while Dabria means the Angel of Death!" She coughed out a laugh that brought up a spittle of blood. "You are an Angel of Death which is a Gift from God." She coughed, again more blood.

Donatella couldn't help but chuckle. Of course, she had heard this on numerous occasions as she was growing up. She countered by saying, "Donatella also has an alternate meaning, 'Beautiful'. So, you can think of me as a Beautiful Angel of Death."

Buckley, smiled, coughed, and spit up blood again. "I like my version better. No one said you were beautiful."

Now it was time for Donatella to muster a laugh. "You're right, Buckley. No one said that at all."

The growing sound of sirens signaled the approach of the emergency vehicles.

"You're going to be okay, Buckley. You're going to make it. And trust me. I will find this bastard and he will pay."

From within the safe, Donatella Dabria retrieved her FBI credentials, her FBI windbreaker, and her FBI issued Sig Sauer P226 9 mm semiautomatic handgun.

The mistake her prey made was that he did not leave town immediately. The fact he had been discovered and had not made a run for it meant he deserved what he had coming to him. Pablo Rodriquez was the gun smuggler Agents Dabria and Buckley had been pursuing just three days prior. After ensuring her partner was safe and out of surgery, Donatella began her search. It took 48 hours for her to locate Rodriquez and another day to devise a plan to get close to him. Pablo was a pig and enjoyed the company of pretty prostitutes. Women that he would beat as part of his sexual fantasy. Donatella didn't have time to play the role of a call-girl, but she knew another thing about Pablo – he liked his spirits. She knew where she could find him and decided to make her move.

Donatella, dressed in fitted dark-blue jeans that hugged the curves of her hips, thigh-high six-inch black leather boots and a white body suit with a severe cut to the cleavage, walked into Frogs Bar and Grill. All heads in the bar swung toward the sound of the door opening and lingered on the sight that was walking through the door. Donatella made her way over to the bar and ordered a drink. She noticed Pablo when she walked through the door but did not make any eye contact. For the first twenty minutes in the bar, she turned away all suitors until approached by Pablo.

"Haven't seen anything you like?" Pablo asked with a cockiness in his tone.

"I haven't seen anything I'm willing to let waste my time," Donatella replied dryly.

"Well I can promise you, I would not be a waste of your time," he said, sitting down on the stool next to her. "You're much too pretty to be in this bar, drinking by yourself. Why don't you let me buy you another?"

"Thanks, but two is my limit for this evening. I simply stopped by on my way home to take the edge off of my day. Now that I've finished..." She tossed back the last of her drink "I'm going to head home and prepare to do it all over again tomorrow."

Recovering quickly, Pablo said, "Well, the world would say chivalry is dead if I don't offer to see you home safely. Why don't I escort you to your building to ensure you arrive unharmed?"

"Look, I appreciate the offer, but I'm sure I can manage, my place is not far from here."

"That makes it even better. With your place being close, you can be rid of me that much sooner."

Finally, Donatella gave in, "Sure."

Pablo left $50 on the bar, nodded to the bartender, and told him to keep the change. The bartender tilted his head forward slightly in appreciation as Donatella and Pablo exited the bar.

Walking west away from the bar, Donatella engaged Pablo in small talk that was meant to keep him disarmed as they approached the second alley down the street. Prior to heading into the establishment, Donatella destroyed the lights that were illuminating this alley. Approaching the mouth of the alley, Donatella exclaimed.

"I think I'm going to be sick!" as she turned to run into the darkness.

Pablo, not wanting his prize to get away, followed Donatella into the alley.

Donatella leaned over, preparing to heave as Pablo walked up directly behind her.

Quickly Donatella pivoted on her right foot, spinning from right to left. She distributed her weight on her right foot as she exploded upward into the solar plexuses of Pablo that both stunned him and sent him flying backward from the unanticipated blow. This wasn't meant to take Pablo down, simply to cause him to momentarily lose his breath long enough for her to snatch the revolver he had tucked in his waistband. Donatella tossed the weapon in the trashcan that was sitting next to her before quickly twisting her hair into a knotted bun.

By this time Pablo had recovered and looked like he was

ready for a fight. He took two quick steps in the direction of Donatella while swinging at her head with a left hook. Sensing the motion more than seeing it completely in the darkness of the alley, she quickly ducked under the attempt and countered with a well-placed strike to the temple. Not waiting to witness the effect the blow would have on his equilibrium, Donatella swung her left leg and connected her foot with Pablo's inner knee. Hearing the satisfying crunch and not waiting on her prey to hit the ground, she followed up with a backhand horizontal chop to the throat. She held back slightly with this blow as she didn't want to crush his windpipe, but she did want him to feel the effects of suffocation as air struggled to make its way through his system. For good measure as he began to fall lifelessly forward, Donatella brought her right knee up quickly to meet his nose, which resulted in a spray of blood on her dark jeans. Within seven seconds the fight, if one could call it that, was over as Pablo lay on the ground.

Thinking she may have gone a bit too far with the breaking of his nose and the slight fracture to his windpipe, she laid Pablo on his back, head tilted to the left with his arms raised above his head as to allow maximum air flow. She couldn't let this bastard die, but she could enjoy the retribution she obtained for her partner.

DONATELLA PLACED her FBI wallet in the front pocket of her freshly creased black trouser pants, placed her Sig Sauer pistol into her black leather shoulder holster, and slipped the windbreaker onto her shoulders. Donatella traced her steps back through the opulent bedroom, down the pair of helix shaped steps in the foyer. She stopped, smelled the

Blue Ocean Breeze Orchids, and walked out of the front door.

It's time to unravel this mystery, Donatella thought as the door clicked shut behind her.

Tuesday, September 17th – 9:30 a.m
Grant Residence (735 Franklin Lane)

SYLVIA GRANT SAT in the room of her son, Thomas Grant, appalled at the secret she had held all of these years and the lengths that she had gone through to keep it from her husband. He was a man she had loved from the moment she first set eyes on him at the gym. The carnal lust she felt watching him as he moved from the rowing machine to the treadmill. She even followed him into the spinning class, though she had never taken spinning a day in her life. But she couldn't just simply let him go without mustering the courage to say hello. The class was nearly the death of her. Ten minutes into the class she realized this was not a leisure ride through the park, which instead involved intense intervals, flashing lights, loud music, and endless motion. By the time the class concluded fifty minutes later, she could barely stand on her legs and stumbled toward the door. Then it happened. This man, the object of her affection, caught her as she stumbled once again reaching for the door to exit the room. He helped her regain her balance and then asked with a baritone voice, "Are you okay, Mrs.?"

Feeling weak in the knees again, and this time not from the riding of the bike, she responded, "Ms! Ms. Turner, and yes, I'm okay. I'd feel better if you could escort me to a seat.

This is the first time I've taken this class, and it's a bit more than I expected."

"Completely understandable. It can be rough the first time through."

"Indeed, it can," she said with a seductive smile as she undressed him visually out of his sweaty clothes.

Understanding her double entendre, he gave her a knowing smile, and they carried on with a more civilized conversation.

But now, at this moment, she hated him. She hated him with every fiber of her being. Yes, she was wrong, and Thomas was living proof of that every single day. But this no-good son of a bitch had slept with her sister. Her sister of all people. Multiple times and in their house. She wanted to scream, throw up, cry in no particular order. She couldn't think of any place in the house that was potentially safe from their embrace, their infidelity. Nowhere other than Thomas's room. *He wouldn't dare do such a horrible, despicable act in the room of their son... well... my son*, she thought.

Mrs. Sylvia Grant was startled out of her daydream by the ringing of the doorbell. She kissed the favorite t-shirt of her son before folding and placing the garment back in his dresser. She wiped the tears that had begun streaming down her face as she made her way to the front door. Composing herself, she swung the door open, and for a moment her chest was caught in her throat.

TUESDAY, SEPTEMBER 17TH – 9:40 A.M
GRANT RESIDENCE (735 FRANKLIN LANE)

"You bitch!" Sylvia Grant snarled with a yell. "Douglas!" she yelled even louder. "How dare you show up to my house? Douglas, call Detective Wilson! Call the police!"

Douglas, sitting in the study as far away from his wife as he could be after his admission from the previous night, was shocked and horrified to hear his wife yelling, swearing, and calling his name. Worried about her safety, he immediately sprung from his seat, left the study, and progressed through the foyer to the front door. His wife, if she would still be that after this ordeal, was standing at the front door visibly shaking. He heard her utter for him to call Detective Wilson and the police, but he was not going to do that until he knew what he was dealing with at the front door.

He passed his wife's shoulder enough to see through the open gap between the door and the door jamb. There he saw the face of Donatella Bianchi. Ushering his wife out of the way, he forcefully jabbed his hand toward her face.

Acting more on reflex than anything else, Special Agent Dabria parried his "attack" and flipped him over her shoulder onto his back.

Douglas was not sure what was happening, he was in the midst of admonishing this child molester who was a suspect in his son's disappearance, and next thing he knew he was seeing the clear blue sky. Dazed and slightly groggy from his fall, he saw the letters "IBF" in yellow on the blue jacket of Donatella.

After being roughly shoved out of the way by her husband, the next sight Sylvia Grant saw was the heels of her husband quickly passing her face. As she reemerged from her exile behind the door and now looking back out into the yard, she saw her husband on the ground looking up at Donatella, who was now hovering over his body. Looking closely at her back, she noticed the letters FBI in big yellow block letters.

What the hell is going on here? Sylvia thought. She noticed Donatella reaching out to her husband.

Still slightly dazed, Douglas Grant reached up to grab the proffered hand. Donatella pulled and within seconds Grant was once again standing on his feet.

Special Agent Dabria finally spoke. "Sylvia, Douglas, do you mind if we go into your house for a word?"

"Are you out of your fucking mind? You have taken our son and now you want to come into our house. Is this some type of sick ransom request? I'm calling the police. I'm calling Detective Wilson. You will be arrested on the spot!"

"That was already tried once today," Donatella said sarcastically. "I assure you it will be a waste of your time, since I did not kidnap your son. It's time we've had a proper introduction. My name is not Donatella Bianchi. In fact, my name is Donatella Dabria. To be more precise, it's Special Agent Donatella Dabria from the Federal Bureau of Investigations."

Both Mr. and Mrs. Grant looked at each other not sure exactly what to say.

"Is this something we can discuss more in depth while sitting in the house?" SA Dabria asked.

Regaining his wits, Douglas said, "Sure, come on in," as he began to walk back to the front door.

"Are you crazy, Douglas? You cannot trust anything that comes out of her mouth. She is a child molester, and she has taken our son."

Wanting the conversation to be over, Agent Dabria pulled her credentials from her pocket, flipped the wallet open, and thrust it into the face of Sylvia Grant. The gold badge and subsequent picture card were displayed for both Sylvia and Douglas to view.

Wanting to hold onto her rage, because she didn't have anywhere else to place it with the disappearance of her son, Sylvia stated. "That's obviously a fake! They would never allow a child molesting kidnapper into the FBI."

Understanding his wife would not relent, Douglas walked through the door and pulled his reluctant wife by the arm. Special Agent Dabria followed through the space left by the Grants, closed, and then locked the front door.

Still fuming after being pulled into the house while standing her ground for her son, Sylvia was ushered down the foyer to sit in the study on the right side of the hall.

The last time I was in this wretched room I had to hear Douglas gloat about sodomizing my twin sister, Sylvia thought as she yanked her arm away from her husband and dropped down into the oversized chair.

Douglas, with furrowed brows, glared over at his wife as she acted like a petulant child. Although Thomas was not his biological son, something he did not come to realize until just recently, inside all he could feel was the love for the boy anyway. As he looked at his wife with ever narrowing eyes, he was quickly deciding this relationship could not and would not last. Her lies, her secrets. His lies, his secrets. They were all squeezed out into the open and there was no stuffing them back into the tube.

Following the Grants into the study, SA Dabria could sense the palpable tension in the room. Honestly, she didn't care about their domestic squabbling unless it could aide her in constructing a picture from the disjointed pieces she had in front of her.

To her knowledge, Thomas Grant and Bree Singleton were not close acquaintances. Sure, they went to the same school, but they had no classes in common. Their families were cordial but did not hang out with each other. Whoever kidnapped these two children were not exhibiting the signs of a discernible "type." In the back of her mind, SA Dabria could only come back to the past of the Singletons, but Thomas's disappearance continued to be the driving factor against that notion. In order for her to make some headway in this fresh investigation, she needed to start with patient zero, Thomas Grant.

"Mr. and Mrs. Grant," she started, "I know you have a number of questions, so let me start by providing some information. As I mentioned at the door, my name is Special Agent Donatella Dabria. I've worked for the Federal Bureau of Investigations for five years. While I cannot give you the specifics of why I'm living in this subdivision and why I took on the persona of a child molester, I can tell you that the disappearance of your son, Thomas, has taken on new a dimension. Earlier today, another child within this subdivision was abducted, Bree Singleton."

"Oh my God!" gasped Sylvia with fear in her eyes as she put her hand to her heart.

Watching the reaction of his wife, Douglas said, "What, Sylvia? Is she another bastard child of Bill's? Maybe he slept with Liz too. Hell, the three of you probably got it on quite well."

"You prick!" Sylvia exclaimed, bolting out of her chair.

With cheetah-like speed, Agent Dabria was between Douglas and Sylvia before Sylvia could land a blow on her husband. "Sit down, Mrs. Grant," Dabria stated firmly.

After a moment of hesitation, Sylvia retraced her steps to her chair and dropped back down.

"Who is Bill and what does he have to do with any of this?" asked Dabria as she sat down in the chair between the Grants.

Not wasting any time, Douglas snarled, "Bill Dresser. He fucked my wife, planted his seed in her fertile womb, and they conceived the child you know as Thomas Grant. If he did it with my wife, he may have done the same with Elizabeth, and now he's working to bring his family together."

This was news for Donatella. She was not aware that Thomas was really the son of Bill Dresser, which would be a line of inquiry she would need to follow up on immediately. Without another word to the Grant's, Agent Dabria stood, walked out of the study, and left through the front door.

Tuesday, September 17th – 10:30 a.m
Thompson Residence (1812 Garden Street)

"Psst Marcellous, don't look now, but isn't that the child molester Bianca, or is it Dionna?" Jasmyn whispered to her husband.

Quickly turning his head to see who his wife was speaking of, Jasmyn exclaimed, "I told you not to look!"

Marcellous, with a sly grin creeping up the corners of his mouth, retorted, "C'mon, Jasmyn. You know dang well when you tell someone not to look at something, looking is the very first thing they are going to do. Furthermore, how am I supposed to confirm if the person you are referring to is in fact a child molester?" He made air-quotes with his fingers.

"Well, look but don't look," Jasmyn replied. "And why is she wearing a windbreaker?"

Attempting to look without looking, Marcellous pinched the bridge of his nose right between the eyes as he turned in his chair, trying to give the nonchalant appearance being deep in thought. When he saw Donatella taking those long strides down the street with both purpose and grace, he gave up the pretense and for a moment simply stared as the figure strolled by without giving him or his wife a glance.

"Pick your mouth up off of your chest." Jasmyn interrupted, bringing Marcellous out of his trance.

"Yeah," he said absentmindedly blinking his eyes back into focus. "That is the one everyone calls the child molester. I believe her name is Donatella."

"That's it!" Jasmyn exclaimed. "I knew it was something like that."

"Sure, because Dionna and Donatella are so close," Marcellous chided sarcastically.

Jasmyn gave him a playful punch on his shoulder, maybe a little harder than necessary to repay for the focus he showed on her striding figure.

"What do you make of that windbreaker?" Jasmyn questioned as the letters became more evident now that she had passed where they were standing.

Missing the yellow letters on the blue jacket the first time because of his mesmerizing trance into her stride, Marcellous took a second look at the departing figure and for the first time noticed the "FBI" lettering on the back of her jacket. "I don't know." He said honestly as he continued to watch her move farther into the distance as each moment passed by. "That is an excellent question. And to top that off, where is she going in such a rush and with such determination? There seems to be more to this woman than we have been led to believe. And who would have ever truly believed she was a child molester? I mean, look at her."

As soon as the words came out of his mouth, Marcellous winced and shrugged his shoulders in defense of the hit he knew was heading his way. After counting to three and not feeling the delicate fist of Jasmyn jab him in the shoulder, he opened his eyes. To his surprise, she had her middle finger tucked behind her thumb. Aiming directly between both of his eyebrows, she released her finger and thumped him squarely between the eyes.

"Ouch!" Marcellous yelped, bringing his hand to his now stinging forehead. "That's going to leave a mark. I may have to call the law for spousal abuse. And it just so happens I see an FBI agent strolling down the street," Marcellous said this with a sly smile on his face. Before his wife could inflict any additional pain, he quickly hopped out of his chair and jumped back two feet.

Jasmyn, one second too slow on the draw, missed the loving haymaker she threw at her husband by mere inches. "You play too much," she said, giving him a glaring look. "You do know I'm going to get you back for this?"

"Girl, you know I lug you. Come on over here and give me some suga." Dropping back into their playful slang brought a smile to Jasmyn's face, and Marcellous walked over, gave her a hug, and slapped a wet kiss right on her cheek.

Tuesday, September 17th – 10:30 a.m
Dresser Household (1135 Milton Court)

"Hey babe, I'm starving, what are we doing for brunch?" asked Diane Dresser as she made her way down the stairs and went straight toward the kitchen. "Matter of fact, how about we put on some clothes and head over to the country club? They have a pecan-crusted chicken salad with balsamic vinaigrette dressing that is the best in the city."

"Di, I'm ten steps ahead of you," Bill responded coyly. "Well, ten steps ahead of your hunger that is."

As Diane turned the corner into their gourmet kitchen, there stood Bill in his white apron, chef's hat, and a determined look on his face. In his right hand he held the red-handled knife sharpener and in his left hand he held the well-balanced red chef's knife. Pressing the sharpener against the right side of the knife with one fluid motion, Bill slid the sharpener across the edge of the blade. Turning his palm skyward to reveal the left side of the chef's knife, he repeated this motion. He alternated this movement five times on each side until the edge of the knife shimmered and was sharp enough to cut a tomato in half with the slightest bit of pressure.

Acknowledging his wife's presence in the room, he continued. "I figured we could munch on some of our favorite finger foods and appetizers. I have prepared for your pallet's delight chilled cured prosciutto rolls with sliced Organic Valley Pepper Jack cheese. We also have softened Philadelphia Original cream cheese topped with Stonewall Kitchen's Hot Pepper Jelly, adorned with Breton gourmet multi-grain crackers. This will be paired with Welch's Sparkling Apple Cider." Bill finished this statement with a bow and a wink.

"Aww hon, this is what I made for you on our very first date," Diane said with a slight blush. "And if I remember correctly, you mister showed up to my house ten minutes late, sweating profusely—*I don't even think it was hot*—carrying flowers I'm sure you took out of Mrs. Wilson's garden. You do know she swore that if she ever found out who trampled through her flower bed and took her prized roses she was going to press charges to the fullest extent of the law. That's all she could talk about for weeks. I think she even put a motion-sensitive camera on her property to watch over her flowers for the rest of her time on this Earth, Lord bless her soul."

"I figured you would like a trip down memory lane,"

Bill said as he loaded a cracker with the cream cheese and pepper jelly mixture. Leaning over toward Diane, he placed the cracker near her mouth. She leaned in the remainder of the way to make up the distance and took a bite.

"Mmm. Delicious!" she said with her eyes rolling to the back of her head in culinary delight. Bill tossed the other half into his mouth, licking the tip of his middle finger clean of the jelly that had landed there during the transfer.

"I'm almost done," Bill stated as he cut a few more slices of cheese. "Why don't you head into the morning room –"

Ding Dong chimed the doorbell from the front door.

Craning her neck to look down the foyer to the glass on the side of the door, Diane asked, "Are you expecting any company?"

"Nope," Bill stated as he continued to slice the cheese wedges.

Eyes now focused down the corridor, though still seated, Diane could see the figure standing in front of the window. Rocking back in her chair to gain the momentum necessary to stand, she could tell the figure's back was to the door. On the back of the jacket she saw at first a single letter, "I." The windowpane obscured the rest of the lettering. However, as her momentum carried her forward out of the chair, the letters "BF" flashed on the jacket. Diane was standing fully on her feet and had taken four steps towards the foyer when what she saw finally registered in her mind.

"Bill, oh my God! It's the FBI. Why is the FBI at our door? Do you think it has anything to do with that missing boy, Thomas Grant?" Slightly hyperventilating and trying yet failing to catch her breath, Diane stood locked in place like a statue.

Bill's jaw tensed and his knuckles became white from

the pressure he exerted on the chef's knife still firmly in his grasp. "Let me go see what they want," Bill stated firmly as he began walking towards the door.

"Not like that you aren't!" Diane exclaimed.

Bill, vexed about the admonishment from his wife, gave her a quizzical look.

"You cannot take that knife to the door with you!"

Bill's subconscious didn't want to relinquish the knife, but he did also untied the apron from behind his back and pulled it over his head, spilling the chef's hat he had forgotten about to the floor. As he made his way to the door, folding the apron into a unified square, he pondered the reason for the FBI appearing at his house. Diane wanted to stay out of the way, but nonetheless she was curious. She stooped down to pick up the hat and placed it on the granite kitchen island. Following in his wake while leering over his shoulder, she too began to ponder the reason for this untimely and unwarranted visit.

Tuesday, September 17th – 10:30 a.m
Driftwood Springs Neighborhood

DONATELLA DABRIA TRAVERSED the streets of Driftwood Springs, trying to find a concrete thread to follow.

Two disappearances, both kids within the same neighborhood and from the same school within a short period of time. Not only was this unheard-of but highly improbable. Thomas Grant, the first child abducted, from the family of Douglas and Sylvia Grant. Well at least the son of Sylvia

Grant. Last seen leaving Josh's house where they were playing basketball.

Picking up the pace and fully striding with her long athletic legs, Special Agent Dabria sensed a pair of eyes cast in her direction. Utilizing the peripheral vision she honed over the years, she could tell those eyes watching her belonged to Jasmyn Thompson. This was soon confirmed when she noticed the quick turn from her husband Marcellous just before being yanked back in the direction from which he had started. *Young love*, she distractedly thought before allowing her mind to sink back into deep contemplation.

The second child, Bree Singleton, was kidnapped on her way to school. Last seen by her parents when she left the house. Abducted while I was being held in police custody under the bogus pretense of kidnapping Thomas Grant. Aside from attending the same school and living in the same neighborhood, the two didn't seem to have any points of intersection.

Again, she came back to the core facts. Two disappearance, both kids within the same neighborhood, from the same school within a short period of time. Not only were the odds unheard-of and improbable, they were impossible. In following this thread, a question lingered on the precipice of her mind. *Does someone know?*

As this thought, this question, bubbled to the forefront of her mind, she realized she was at the home of Bill and Diane Dresser. She casually reached out and pressed the doorbell and heard the report from within the structure of the house. Hearing the rustle of what sounded like footsteps, she executed a 180 degree turn to check her flank and realized it was a pair of twins making their way down the street. Absentmindedly she mused, *aren't they supposed to be in school*? Nonetheless, they were of no concern of hers, unless they too came up missing, though she was confident this would not be the case.

She could hear the footfalls cautiously approaching from within the house. Detective Dabria turned around just as the door swung open.

"Yes, how can we –" the remainder of the question caught in the throat of Bill Dresser when he realized the figure standing before him was Donatella Bianchi, the child molester.

"What the hell are you doing here?" he asked with a snarl. "And why in the holy hell are you impersonating an FBI agent?"

"Bill, what's wrong? Who is it?" Diane asked as her steps slowed, coming to the side of her husband. "You!" she nearly barked, eyes narrowing, pupils blazing, eyebrows tightening. "What are you –"

"Diane," Bill interrupted. "Call Detective Wilson. Let him know the child molester is not only trespassing but impersonating an FBI agent. I'm sure he'll be appalled and delighted at the same time. He's been waiting for you to fuck up," he said, glaring at Donatella. "And you have certainly stepped in it now."

"Yes," Agent Dabria said in her Southern drawl. "Mrs. Dresser, do go and call Detective Wilson. I saw him as I departed the Grant's abode on my way to visit you. And surely take your time. This will give me and Bill here a few moments to chat undisturbed before you return."

Taken aback, Diane's eyes narrowed to the point they were nearly closed, the fire within those eyes intensified and her brow became nearly rock solid. Uncertain of her next action, Diane stood there frozen and looked to her husband for guidance.

Bill, a man who was prone to read both people and situations, began to feel uneasy about the situation that lay before him and his wife. Staring into the hazelnut eyes of Donatella, he sensed no trace of apprehension, and this worried him. Within the span of ten seconds, she mentioned the Grants, the fact she relished speaking with him alone, and she had just passed Detective Wilson on her way to their house. Surely if this was true, he would have already seen her in the FBI windbreaker. If so, there was more to this situation that he did not know, and until he could figure out exactly what that something was he didn't want his wife around to hear the words that would come from the mouth of this woman.

"Hon," he said with a voice of finality. "I'll speak with Ms. Bianchi."

"But Bill!" Diane began to protest.

"It's okay," he reassured her with a kiss on the cheek. "I'll step out here onto our porch to see what she has to say. You mentioned you had a ravenous hunger when you came down the stairs. Why don't you head back into the kitchen, pop open the sparkling cider, and pull down a few glasses."

"But Bill!" she persisted.

"I'll be in shortly," he continued, "and we can complete the recreation of our first date."

Agent Dabria internally rolled her eyes.

Looking uncomprehendingly at her husband and unsure what just happened, she said, "Okay." Her voice was shaking ever so slightly as she retreated from the doorway and back into the house.

Tuesday, September 17th – 10:35 a.m
Dresser Residence (1135 Milton Court)

DIANE, scurrying towards the kitchen to leave her husband and Donatella out front, reached her ringed hand into her pants pocket and retrieved her cell phone. She raised her Samsung Galaxy S10 to her face to activate the facial recognition software thus unlocking her phone. Once complete, she scrolled through her list of contacts until she found the one she was looking for and dialed. Of course, this was not a hard feat, since she'd dialed this number so many times before. Anticipating the duration of time she had to chat would be short, she willed the phone to ring and the person on the other side to pick up.

One ring, two rings, three rings. She began to feel this was a mistake to call this early and also the feeling of rejection if the line was not answered. As she began to lose hope and awaited the voicemail to activate after the fourth ring, the phone was answered.

"Hello," the voice said on the other end of the phone.

Diane could hear the faint trail of footsteps in the background once the phone was answered. She figured this would be the case and in her own mind, she didn't care. She expected the phone to be answered when she placed the call.

In a jumble of words, she began, "Donatella Bianchi just arrived at our house asking to speak with me and Bill. Bill advised me to call Detective Wilson, figuring this would put a scare into her, but you know what, she dared me to do it. Matter of fact she damn near begged me to do it. Infuriated and about to give her a piece of my mind, Bill stopped me in mid-sentence. Then he basically shooed me away so that he could talk with her alone. I received a weird vibe between those two that I couldn't articulate then, but I think I have a clue now. Honestly, I don't know why I hadn't seen it before. He's sleeping with that trollop, that slut, that child molester!" The last word was uttered with pure venom.

Diane continued, "But that is perfectly fine if he is dipping his wick in that, that, that bitch! With her silky-smooth skin, firm breasts, round ass. If that is the case, he can have her. He can have her! That just means that you and I can now be together. This is the moment we have been waiting for over the last year. A way for me out of this union he and I share. Douglas, I love you. We can do this. Tell me we can do this, that we will do this."

On the other end of the line, Douglas Grant, now seated in his study, responded, "Diane, I love you too, but there is more to this story than you know. How much of the conversation with Donatella did you overhear?"

Dumbfounded why he had a calm, measured voice and why he wasn't as excited at this opportunity as she was, Diane answered her secret lover. "I didn't hear any of the conversation. Bill asked me to make my way back into the house and wait in the kitchen. That's when I figured I would seize the moment to call you. I figured that wife of yours would be around, but I knew you would take my call."

Douglas responded cautiously. "Diane, there is something you need to know. There are several things you need to know actually. Donatella was just at our house and –"

"Yeah!" Diane said, interrupting. "She said she was just

leaving your house and ran into Detective Wilson as she was leaving. And what's the deal with this fake FBI jacket she is wearing. In fact, as soon as I finish with you, can you put Detective Wilson on the phone if he is still there? Matter of fact, don't do that. I don't need to have Sylvia wondering why I called your phone. I could always say it was to offer any assistance in finding Thomas, though she would wonder why I didn't call her."

Douglas, growing impatient with her rambling, raised his voice, "Damn it, Diane. Be quiet and listen. The woman at your house, the woman we have all known as Donatella Bianchi, is not who we all thought her to be when she moved into Driftwood Springs. She truly is an FBI agent."

Diane let out an audible gasp while covering her mouth.

"I'm not sure why she is in our subdivision and why she put on this charade, but this is something I confirmed with Detective Wilson when he stopped by our house. As it turns out another child, Bree Singleton, has disappeared, and she had questions on how well Thomas and Bree may have known one another. However, Diane, there is something more important you should know. It's about Thomas."

"Oh my God, Doug! How insensitive could I be? How is the hunt for your son going? How are you holding up? How can I help you?"

"God damn it, Diane! Thomas is not my son. He is not my son. He, he," Douglas could feel his blood pressure escalating. "Your husband is Thomas's biological father!"

Tuesday, September 17th – 10:40 a.m
Grant Residence (735 Franklin Lane)

SYLVIA GRANT COULD HEAR the hushed conversation coming from the study. She was curious who Doug could be speaking with, but she dared not press the issue. At this moment, her heart still ached for the loss of her son. She didn't want to think of it as a loss, because she knew he was still out there. She would've known if he were no longer living. That maternal bond would tell her that something happened to him if something did happen to him. Yet that maternal bond failed her when he was taken. Wasn't he in danger then? How was it that she didn't feel harm coming his way at that moment? Grasping for her phone from within her robe, Sylvia pulled up her messaging app. She needed to get a message to Bill, but she didn't want Diane to stumble across his phone and begin to wonder.

"Call me!" she typed into the app. However, before pushing send, she thought of the question he would receive from Diane if she were to read this. She erased and started again.

"We need to talk." Hell, that was no better. Again, she deleted it.

She could have sworn she heard the word Diane come out of Douglas's study. She mused that was made up in her mind since she was thinking about Diane at that moment.

Taking a few more moments to contemplate, she typed, "Doug and I could use some close friends nearby to help comfort us after the disappearance of our son." Maybe he would understand the "our son" part. Just then, from the study in an elevated voice she heard, "God damn it, Diane!" This time she knew it wasn't made up in her head.

Douglas's voice went back to a whisper after uttering those words.

Could there be another Diane? Surely, he wouldn't be talking to Diane Dresser. Then again, why wouldn't he be speaking to her? He just found out her husband was the father of their son... her son. Surely, he could feel their marriage was ruined, likely was ruined, and he was hell-bent on destroying their marriage too. Douglas wasn't a spiteful, vengeful man, but then again when pushed too far, she never knew what someone will do.

Erasing the message once again, she wrote, "He knows... and likely so does your wife!" and pressed send.

Tuesday, September 17th – 10:40 a.m
Dresser Residence (1135 Milton Court)

DABRIA TOOK a step back and to the side to allow Bill to pass through the doorway onto the porch. Once cleared, he pulled the door behind him until the latch made an audible click as it settled into place.

"Before I ask any questions and you prepare to lie to me," Agent Dabria stated, her hazelnut eyes fixed on Bill. "I want you to understand I know more than you are willing to share or confirm. So, let's clear the air and start off on the right foot. My name is Special Agent Donatella Dabria with the FBI. While you know me as Donatella Bianchi, I have been working, let us say undercover from the moment I first arrived in Driftwood Springs. The nature of my work is of no importance to you at this moment, but there are developments that require me to break cover and address the situation head on. Are you following me, Bill?"

Dresser nodded his head in affirmation.

Agent Dabria continued. "You are the father of Thomas Grant, am I correct?"

"Well," Bill began to stammer. "That's not...who told you such a –"

"Bill," Agent Dabria interrupted with a sardonic tone. "I said you would want to lie to me, and to be honest I don't have the patience to play games. We can wait until Diane's curiosity to know why you sent her away gets the best of her and she appears back at the door. I give her three minutes. But understand this, you will answer my questions with or without her present. The choice is yours. Father, yes or no?"

Bill quickly calculated his options. "Yes," he blurted, dropping his head a few degrees.

"Do you know of any reason anyone would want to hurt him or for that matter Mr. or Mrs. Grant?"

"None. Thomas was always a good boy. He's well-liked by everyone in this neighborhood and has a good deal of friends at school. He has a good head on his shoulders and continuously practices personal security. I recall one day the rain was pounding on us here. I was on my way home from the grocery store and saw Thomas walking with haste toward his house. I pulled over to ask if he wanted a ride and he declined. He knows our families are close, and he knows me. For him to refuse a ride in those conditions, you can tell he was raised right."

Dabria considered this and pressed forward. "Does anyone beside Sylvia and you know the truth about

Thomas's paternity?" She purposefully neglected to mention Sylvia's husband was now aware.

"No!" Bill stated in a rush. "And I would prefer to keep it that way. If Diane were to discover the truth, it would likely mean the end of our marriage. Likewise, for Sylvia I would imagine."

"Do you have any reason to believe Thomas would run away? Could he have possibly discovered the truth about his true parents?"

Bill vehemently shook his head in response to each question.

"Last question, where were you at the time of Thomas's disappearance?"

The distant eyes that had overcome Bill in the previous set of questions had now taken on a razor-sharp edge.

"Do you think I had something to do with his disappearance? That is absurd. I would never, NEVER do anything to jeopardize his well-being. If you really must know, I was at home with Diane, my wife!" Bill stated for emphasis.

"An alibi I'm sure you don't want confirmed with your wife," SA Dabria stated with a hint of sarcasm.

Before Bill could respond, the wooden door with the decorative glass inlay swung open. "What is she still doing here?" Diane asked.

"Nothing, dear," Bill countered as he completed a half turn so that he could see both his wife and the Special Agent. "Donatella was just about to leave. Isn't that right?" He flashed a cold glare.

"Yes, I was just about to leave. Should I have any follow-up questions, I'll be sure to stop by again." With that, she turned on her heel, walked down the stairs, and began the walk back to her place.

Returning into their house, Bill felt the phone in his pocket vibrate. Allowing his wife to take the lead in front of him, he pulled the phone out of his pocket and looked down at the screen. With his right hand on the phone, his left hand reached behind him to push the door shut. When his eyes focused on the screen, he saw the message. "He knows... and likely so does your wife!" He unlocked the phone, deleted the message, and placed the phone back into his pocket.

TUESDAY, SEPTEMBER 17TH – 5:00 P.M
UNDISCLOSED LOCATION

H*eadline: Kidnapper strikes again? Suspect detained? More questions than answers*
www.TheSalReport.com

By: Sal Grandson

The community of Driftwood Springs has been marred again with tragedy as another child has disappeared. Detective Wilson has stopped short of categorizing the disappearance as kidnappings or even linking the two disappearances. However, there are similarities that cannot be overlooked. Both children attended the same school, both disappeared within the confines of the gated community, a community in which Detective Wilson resides, and both have no history of disappearing before. Though the police are not willing to describe both as kidnappings, the vibe and conversation around the community supports that claim.

The police detained one of the residents from within the community as a potential suspect late Monday evening. The person detained was Donatella Bianchi. Bianchi, a registered child molester, moved into the Driftwood Springs neighborhood roughly three months ago to the dismay of the residence. A petition was filed with the county, but no action could be taken to remove her from her dwellings. Bianchi's detainment was short-lived, as she was seen leaving Police HQ the following morning, driven away in an FBI vehicle. She was not being detained by the FBI, and Detective Wilson, who was seen leaving HQ shortly after Bianchi, would not discuss the reason for her swift departure.

Where are the missing children of Driftwood Springs? Do we have a potential serial kidnapper on our hands? What's the mystery behind Donatella Bianchi, and what does she have to do with this case? Certainly, more questions than answers, but as I unravel the clues, I'll be sure to keep you, the reading public, well-informed.

Tuesday, September 17th – 5:30 p.m
Singleton Residence (315 Calgary Lane)

THE INSIDE of the Singleton household, filled with two occupants, was coffin quiet. Elizabeth Singleton, curled in a white Kennedy Barrel oversized chair covered with a Dante throw blanket, gazed glass-eyed at a picture of Bree. Her mind was hundreds of miles away, trying to pinpoint how they got to this point. Eyes scarlet red and puffy from the hours of crying, she was now saddled with a migraine headache. The kind that felt like two vice grips straddling the outer edge of her eyeballs, and with each passing moment there was a quarter-inch turn to the right. She stopped looking at the picture frame hours ago, but holding the frame gave her purpose, focus. To what end this gave her the aforementioned she was not sure, but this was what she has, and she would not let it go.

Mr. Singleton too was in deep thought. However, his thought process was singular, kill the son of a bitch who had taken his daughter, his baby girl, the key to his heart. Use all resources available to him and have them beg for everlasting mercy. The only problem? He had no resources and had never even killed an insect. Well, that was not totally true. He or mainly his wife and by virtue of their marriage had Donatella on his side. She was someone he could trust, and she was someone he knew could take care of business. He began to think back to the first time he met Donatella. It was a Fourth of July cookout his wife had thrown prior to them getting married.

Donatella and his wife had known each other since they were kids. In fact, they lived in the same neighborhood, and the back of their houses faced one another. Donatella's mom would babysit his wife when her parents had an outing. They were inseparable, those two. The babysitting turned into sleepovers, and the sleepovers turned into all-night jam sessions singing 90s boy band songs until their hearts were content. His wife lamented how simple life was prior to Donatella losing her parents. Everything changed, as one would expect. She had to move in with her aunt, and for a time they lost touch. It wasn't until the two were in college that they were able to reconnect.

A ringing phone broke Frank's thoughts, and he stood up and made his way over to it. Elizabeth watched him wearily with the feeling of a boulder at the bottom of her stomach.

"Hello," Frank uttered cautiously.

"Mr. Singleton, or should I say Mr. Hartley?" the voice on the other end of the phone asked.

Frank's eyes shifted to his wife, and she too met his.

The voice continued, "Be a dear, Frank, and put me on speaker so your wife can hear me too. I only plan to say this once and I want to make sure you are both crystal clear."

Frank pressed the speaker button located on the phone and increased the volume two clicks so his wife could hear as well.

"We are both here."

"Good," he said, elongating the single syllable word. "You two are some slippery little devils and I don't fancy working this hard to complete a job."

"Where is my daughter, you monster?" yelled Elizabeth, raising swiftly from her chair.

"Tisk, tisk, Mrs. Hartley, it's not nice to call names. No need to be ugly when we are having a civilized conversation. But rest assured, she is safe and will stay that way as long as you do what you are told. Now, my employer has informed me you are meant to testify against his firm on Monday September 23rd, and this is something we just cannot have. You are going to refuse to go through with the testimony. Let's call it a case of amnesia. You forgot everything you were going to say. Also, you will not involve Special Agent Dabria. We know you have a long history with her. Here's a shocker. I do too. But that is a different story for a different day. For now, your focus should be on doing nothing – absolutely nothing. You do that and not one hair will be harmed on Bree's pretty little head.

However, should you disobey my directive. Well, let's just say you will not disobey my directive. And to ensure you play by my rules and to provide you some additional motivation, I suggest you turn to your local CBS affiliate. I have a sneaky suspicion they are going to have some breaking news relatively soon. Ta Ta!"

The phone went dead. Before Frank could return the receiver to the base, Elizabeth had the remote in her hand, and the room became illuminated with lights burning from the TV screen. Frantically Elizabeth flipped through the channels until she landed on CBS. At that moment there was an infomercial selling a knife that could cut through a cement block. Elizabeth could sense Frank's eyes on her, but she didn't turn to meet them. *Was there going to be some news about Bree on the screen. Were they going to say something about her baby?* Her migraine had been pushed aside by her will to concentrate on whatever was going to happen.

Suddenly the infomercial was interrupted with the "Breaking News" intro music as the words materialized on the screen like a bad PowerPoint animation. Unconsciously, Elizabeth Hartley was holding her breath while simultaneously squeezing the remote in her hand. Once the music concluded, the anchorwoman, Susan Richardson, began.

"Good evening. We have breaking news regarding the disappearance of the children from the Driftwood Springs community. On the scene we have Graham Lawson. Graham, what can you tell us?"

"Well, Susan, I'm here at the construction site for Orbitz Technology's new campus on Martin Luther King Boulevard. The campus is meant to provide under-privileged youths the opportunity to learn about science, technology, engineering, math. The core components in the STEM initiatives. Orbitz is also adding the components for artificial intelligence, virtual reality, and robotics. However, on this evening it's with a heavy heart that I'm reporting a body of a young child has been found. In the background you can see the police and forensic scientists working diligently to uncover any clues that may remain."

"Graham, you mentioned this may be related to the disappearance of Thomas Grant and Bree Singleton. Have the police confirmed that the body on the site belongs to either one of the children?"

"Susan, they have not. However, renowned journalist Sal Grandson, who has been following this story closely, was the one who discovered the body. But as you will hear from the taped interview we did just before coming on air, it seems he had some unlikely assistance."

Rolling the already queued clip, the unwavering Grandson appeared on the screen and began to speak. "Graham, I received a call roughly an hour ago telling me I could find Thomas Grant at Orbitz Technology's new facility. Thinking this to be some perverse joke, since this is the location of his father, Douglas Grant's, new technology campus, I immediately discounted the call. But the journalist in me nagged that I needed to follow-up all leads, so I made my way over here to the construction site. After a few minutes of walking the exterior grounds and seeing no trace of any remains, I was about to head home. That was until I noticed the large industrial dumpsters. Walking thirty paces to the dumpster, I continued to think this was a waste of time. Nonetheless, I found a foothold and climbed up so I could take a better look at the contents inside. This was when I spotted a body laying within the debris. Unfortunately, the body had its back to me. Quickly I jumped down, sprinted over to the other side and climbed the dumpster again. When I did, the lifeless eyes of Thomas Grant were staring back at me."

'What did you do next?" asked Graham.

"My first call was to the police. I gave them my name, location, and what I had found. My second call was to Lisa, your producer, to let her know there was a break in the case. My final call was to the Lord to bless his soul."

The video froze on Grandson's last word and the feed kicked back over to Graham. After a few seconds delay, Graham chimed in, "Susan, while we still await the official word from the police, it seems likely that for one family this disappearance has had a disastrous ending. Back to you."

"Thanks, Graham," Susan Richardson said as the live feed focused back on her now solemn expression. Elizabeth Hartley turned off the television, plunging the room back into the cacophonous silence that occupied the house before that call came into their household. A call that was now forcing their hands and endangering the effort to bring their daughter back home.

Tuesday, September 17th – 7:00 p.m
Undisclosed Location

DONATELLA TOOK the news concerning the death of Thomas Grant harder than she thought she would. She had not been working the case directly, but she still felt responsible for his death. Though she liked to work cases out in her head, she felt there were times when bouncing ideas off of someone else could shed light on a difficult case. She thought back on her decision to officially cut ties with her partner.

"Sir, do you have a moment? I have a personnel question I would like to discuss with you."

"Sure," answered Senior Special Agent John Brewer. SSA Brewer had been an agent in the FBI for the last thirty-five years. Although he had plenty of spunk left within him for the job, his wife Nancy wanted him home for dinner every night. She wanted them to begin taking the trips around the globe he promised her when they first married. He started his career with the bureau out of the Ohio field office at the age of twenty-five. During his ten years in Ohio, Agent Brewer would be the first to admit he had not seen a lot of excitement. For Nancy, the lack of excitement was to her liking, because she felt this kept John safe. However, he felt quite differently, and the slow movement of his cases had him contemplating a change in careers. The day he decided he would give it one more year, his superior approached him with a proposition.

"Brewer, we have an opportunity in the North Carolina field office for a Special Agent with your skill set and determination. Someone who can run the agents down there and ensure the team is held accountable. Are you our man, Brewer?"

Agent Brewer immediately allowed the word "yes" to flow from his lips before considering what his wife would think about this move. He had heard a great deal about the NC field office. Their cases, while not legendary, were a marked improvement to the cases he had been assigned in the Ohio field office.

Special Agent Brewer sold Nancy about the move to North Carolina, where the temperature and the four seasons appealed to her. The move was everything that Brewer hoped for and more. He worked on compelling cases one after another. Under his leadership, he was able to turn the office into one of the more well-respected field offices in the bureau.

Then came this rookie right out of the academy, Donatella Dabria. He could tell she had what was needed to be a phenomenal top-notch agent, but he could also tell she had a chip on her shoulder. He studied her background, read about the tragedy that had taken her parents, and knew she used this as fuel to drive her to excel. It was clear she had an agenda, and he was willing to give her some rope, but not at the expense of the bureau. She would be an agent he had to keep a close eye on while she was under his command.

Agent Dabria continued, "Well sir, Agent Buckley will be moving back to the active roster soon, and to be honest I've become accustomed to working my cases solo."

"There are reasons why we pair agents, especially new agents –"

"I know," she interrupted. "However, you have to admit my record has been exemplary. I produce and there is no dis –"

"I agree your record speaks for itself. In time, I believe you will be one of the best agents I have worked with, but you need to understand that being an agent is not about self."

"I get that, sir. It's about getting the job done and doing what we can to protect those who cannot always protect themselves. Nonetheless, I think having a partner, especially Terri, will only slow me down from getting the job done."

She felt in her heart that Agent Buckley didn't have what it took to be a good agent, and some decisions she made in the field were reckless. If she was going to be saddled with a partner, she needed one she could trust, and as of late she found it hard to trust Agent Buckley. She continued to drive home point after point until finally Special Agent Brewer relented. She could continue running her solo acts, but if her cases began to suffer in any way this arrangement would need to be revisited.

Sitting in the dark, eyes adjusting to her surroundings, Special Agent Dabria allowed these recollections to flow unabated through her mind. Her record was spotless. Every case that she worked was solved, one way or another. She was determined that the case with the Hartley's would not be her first failure. Not because of her perfect record, but because Frank, Liz, and Bree trusted her. She assured them that she could do this alone, and they believed in her more than they believed in the system. She would not, could not let them down. She needed to find Bree and to put this madness to an end.

She heard footsteps approaching, *Finally*.

Tuesday, September 17th – 7:00 p.m
Grandson Residence (4208 Jasper Road)

SAL, a hardened reporter from New York City, was grief stricken by the sight he uncovered at the Orbitz Technology

Campus. For all the bad in this world, no child should ever have to feel its effects. Looking through eyes that were now filling with tears, Sal found it hard to insert the key into the lock. After several attempts, he inserted the key and unlocked the door with a flick of his wrist. Sal, passing over the threshold of his home, felt he needed to leave the day behind him on the outside of the door. He took a deep breath, closed his eyes, and exhaled slowly while counting. *1, 2, 3, 4, 5*. Once he reached 5, he closed the door with his mind clear, placed his bag in the chair next to the door, and turned on the light. Sal made a right-hand turn into the kitchen and headed straight for the refrigerator. He pulled out an ice-cold beer, placing the bottle to his head and reveling in the cold bottle against his brow.

"Ah," exalted Sal. "Just what I needed." Sal left the kitchen and headed to his living room to watch some mindless television. Sal turned the knob on the end table lamp twice to the right, illuminating the room.

"Good evening, Sal," came the voice from across the room.

Sal found himself scared shitless, his heart rate raising to a rhythm he hadn't heard since he ran the half-marathon in Boston. A run he had to do as the result of a bet he lost involving a game between the Boston Red Sox and the New York Yankees. He had two options for how he could pay off the bet. His first option was he could wear a Boston Red Sox jersey to the next Yankees home game. Sal absolutely refused and said he would not put on that jersey if his life depended on it. His second option was he could go over to Boston and run in the Boston Marathon. He would only need to run the half, and he had a year until he would need to pay up on the bet. Though neither option appealed to

Sal, he decided the half-marathon was the lesser of two evils. He had trained, or at least he felt he trained, yet his body was in full revolt by the time he reached the finish line.

"Come in and have a seat," the voice continued, causing another increase in his already-pounding heart. "No need to worry. I'm just here to talk and obtain some answers."

The voice certainly didn't sound menacing, and in fact it had a soothing Southern twang that was indigenous to the area. Recovering his wits, he was now able to focus on the uninvited visitor to his home. *My God! She is absolutely gorgeous* was the first thought that ran through his mind.

"My name is Donatella Dabria."

Sal quickly ran through his mental Rolodex, but the name could not fight its way to the forefront of his mind. He had the sensation of the name being on the tip of his tongue, but no matter how much he tried it wasn't ringing a bell. The only Donatella he knew, or make that the only Donatella he had heard of, was Donatella Bianchi. The woman who was arrested by the police, released, and hurried off in an FBI vehicle. Intrigued and realizing she didn't have any weapon pointed at him, he decided to take the seat next to the lamp he had just turned on.

The visitor continued, "For clarity, I'm Special Agent Donatella Dabria with the FBI." She reached her right hand towards the small of her back, and Sal felt his heart momentarily stop. Since when did the FBI appear in his house unannounced? This had to be a ruse and she was indeed about to kill him, just as he let his guard down. As her hand moved from behind her back, he flinched but did not take his eye off of this woman. What she pulled from behind her back was a wallet, that she unceremoniously flipped open, displaying her credentials and her badge.

Sal took a quick look at the credentials and then again at the woman sitting across from him in his living room. Still apprehensive, he relented and asked, "How can I help you, Special Agent Dabria?"

Dabria folded her credentials and placed the wallet in her pocket. With measured words she stated, "You wrote the first article about the disappearance of Thomas Grant. You were the first one to write about my arrest with the police and subsequent release on the grounds that I worked for the FBI. Tonight, you were the first one on the scene to uncover the body of Thomas Grant. How is that Sal? How are you just so lucky to be in the right place at the right time, all the time?"

Sal blinked his eyes twice in an effort to focus his brain. "I wouldn't exactly call it luck, well maybe some of it was luck. I have friends who live in Driftwood Springs. I was visiting them at their home when the first disappearance happened. Although they had locked down the neighborhood, I was already on the inside and decided to take advantage of my luck." Sal said the last word with emphasis. "The next two were indeed curious. I received an email telling me that a Donatella Bianchi had been arrested as a potential suspect in the disappearance of Thomas Grant and that she would likely be released soon."

At this Donatella interrupted Sal's story. "Wait... repeat that one more time."

"I received an email stating that a Donatella Bianchi had been arrested as a potential suspect in the disappearance of Thomas Grant and that she would likely be released soon." Sal repeated with a tone of curiosity.

How did someone know that I had been arrested, and what made them believe I would be released? This call would not have originated from the FBI. Donatella couldn't make sense of this information, yet urged Sal to continue. "What about the body? How is it that you knew where the body was located?"

"I received a call. A call that said I could find Thomas Grant at the Orbitz Technology Campus. I honestly didn't believe it was true, but I had to go take a look. I wish it had not been true," Sal whispered under his breath, eyes now downcast.

"Who called you, Sal?" asked SA Dabria.

"I'm not sure. The caller made the statement and immediately disconnected the call."

Dabria pondered this for a moment, hands steepled and eyes closed. The silence lingered long enough that Sal began to wonder if she had fallen asleep. He then broke the silence.

"Oh, on the email I received, the sender mentioned one more thing."

SA Dabria lowered her hands and opened her eyes.

"The email mentioned that there had been a second disappearance."

"A second disappearance?!" Dabria called, raising her eyebrow.

"Yeah. The email said another child from the same community was now missing. This all seemed a little farfetched at the time, but nonetheless I decided to make my way to the police station. Just when I began to believe there wasn't anything to glean from the station, your pals in their big black vehicles pulled up. You walked out the door shortly thereafter and hopped into the front seat of the vehicle. At the time I was still under the impression your last name was Bianchi." Sal gave a pause after this last bit waiting to see if Donatella would provide some context on why she was known as Bianchi when her last name was indeed Dabria. After a few moments he realized no additional information was forthcoming, so he continued. "I began to make my way over to the HQ building where I came face to face with Detective Wilson. I grilled him on the possible second disappearance, which he eventually confirmed before storming off in his vehicle. This became the basis of my next article."

"Detective Wilson confirmed the disappearance of the second child? Did he provide any information on the child other than the fact the child was missing from the same community?"

"He just mentioned the two cases would be treated as separate cases, and he was on the way to speak with the families." Sal responded. He noticed a grave expression pass over the facial features of Donatella.

"Sal," Donatella stated as she began to stand, thus imparting upon Sal that he should stand as well. "If you receive any additional information about this case from anonymous sources, I ask that you share them with me before they go any further. There is more at stake than you know. I cannot get into those things now, but I ask that you do this for me."

Sal wanted to ask more, but something told him he should not. He would not gain any more information if Donatella didn't will it so. He nodded his head in acquiescence and shook the hand she had extended.

9

TUESDAY, SEPTEMBER 17TH – 10:00 P.M
DETECTIVE WILSON'S RESIDENCE (407 PARK LANE)

Detective Wilson sat in the family room of his brick two-story Toll Brothers home on Park Lane, watching the recording of Monday Night's football game between the Pittsburgh Steelers and the Carolina Panthers. With the excitement of the last few days he needed this three-hour distraction, or a little over two hours if he fast-forwarded through commercials. Afterward he would plunge back into his cases. Ever since Wilson was a kid, Monday Night football felt like a celebration to him. With Al Michaels on the play-by-play and Frank Gifford adding the color commentary, every match up felt like it was the match up of the decade and tonight would be a real treat. Even though he grew up in New York, he had always been a Steelers fan, and as they say Steelers fans are everywhere. Looking down at his terrible towel that had been signed by "Mean" Joe Greene, he settled in for the kickoff and took a swig of his Coca-Cola in homage to his favorite childhood player. Over the years the team had changed, but their lunchpail workmanship attitude still ran through the core of the team.

Placing his drink into the cup holder on the reclined theater seat, Wilson picked up the remote and pressed play. The special teams from both teams began to make their way onto the field. The Panthers had won the toss but had deferred to the second half, thus his beloved Steelers would be on offense first. Unless, they took the opening kickoff back for a touchdown, which would be a fantastic way to start the game or Lord forbid they turned the ball over on the kickoff thus giving the Panthers an early gift. The place kicker raised his right hand above his head, signaling he was ready to kick the ball. He looked to his left and then again to his right to ensure his teammates were ready – he began his approach.

Ding Dong bellowed the sound of the doorbell. Wilson paused the game with the ball suspended at its apex framed perfectly in the middle of the screen. *Who could this be?* Wilson pondered as he made his way through the foyer to the front door. Taking a quick peek through the side window, he was shocked to see who had made an appearance. He opened the door. "Agent Dabria, what can I do for you this evening?"

"I hope I'm not disturbing you, Detective Wilson, but we need to chat. Do you mind if I come in?"

"Can't this wait until the morning when this can be discussed down at HQ?"

"Ahh." Agent Dabria demurred in her familiar Southern Drawl "Two children are missing from within your own neighborhood and you want to wait until morning." She said this while raising an eyebrow. "A neighborhood, a gated neighborhood, in which the residents would think they are safe, especially with a chief detective living amongst them. Yet right from under your nose two children were snatched, one now presumed dead, and you would like to wait until morning to discuss the merits of the case. Do you really want to put the fate of the other missing child on hold?"

The color in Wilson's face had now risen above his cheeks and began creeping toward his forehead.

"Special Agent Dabria," he finally managed to say, voice crackling with each word. "You, nor the FBI, have any jurisdiction in this case, and if I say it can wait until the morning, then it can wait until the morning." He said, feeling he'd found a perfect loophole to put this woman off and move back to his game.

Not missing a single beat, Agent Dabria countered, "Well, that's where you are wrong, Detective Wilson. With the turn of today's events, I have all the jurisdiction I need. I'm here simply as a matter of course and to inform you to stay out of my way. Now, are you willing to discuss this one professional to another, or do we need to stand here and exchange useless barbs until you realize you are going to give me what I ask for regardless of how much you want to fight against it?"

Reluctantly, Detective Wilson stepped aside so that Agent Dabria could enter his home. They made their way through the foyer back into the family room, where Wilson had begun to watch the Steelers vs Panthers game.

"Detective," Agent Dabria stated when they were seated in the family room. "There is more to this case than the simple disappearances. The Singleton family is in truth the Hartley family and was moved into this community under witness protection."

Wilson gave a look of mild surprise, but did not interrupt Agent Dabria.

"I decided to take on the case of watching over them until their court appearance because of my connection with the family. A job I was doing quite well until you and your partner decided to detain me for no good reason."

"I had very good –"

Donatella stalled the rebuttal from Wilson by putting her hand in the air, forming the universal sign for stop.

"I have every reason to believe the kidnapping of Bree Hartley and the kidnapping of Thomas Grant are connected."

"Now you wait one minute, there is no evidence to prove –"

Dabria shot Wilson a glare that stole the words from his mouth and thoughts from his head.

"I'm confident the people who took Thomas killed him to prove a point to the Hartley's that if they do not back off from this testimony, they will do the same to Bree. In fact, I'm willing to bet they have already made contact with the Hartley's and have warned them of my involvement. Wilson, we are dealing with a sick, sadistic group that would murder innocent children in order to get what they want. My number one job is the safety of the Hartley's, the return of Bree. I hope there will be no interference from the CMPD as I work to ensure the safe return of this girl."

Feeling the need to gain some sort of upper hand, Detective Wilson wanted to say he and his department would not relinquish any portion on this case until her claim could be validated. He desperately wanted to say this. However, the cold, calculating glare from SA Dabria had him second guessing what he wanted to say and what he knew he should say. Not accustomed to being handled in this manner, every fiber of his being wanted to reach out and strangle this woman, but again what he wanted to do and what he would do were at odds.

"We will stay out of your way for now." He said, gritting his teeth.

"Splendid!" Agent Dabria said as she stood from her chair.

Wilson began to stand as well.

"No need to stand. I can see my way out." As she left the family room, she spoke over her shoulder. "The Steelers lose the game on a last second Hail Mary."

Tuesday, September 17th – 11:00 p.m
Undisclosed Location

"I UNDERSTAND you had a visit today from Special Agent Dabria," the voice stated flatly and with no trace of emotion.

"Indeed we did. She's been a busy little bee visiting with all manner of people."

"We have a lot riding on the outcome of this trial. We cannot afford for Frank Hartley to testify. Is she any closer to unraveling the case?" asked the voice.

"I don't think so."

"We did not bring you into this enterprise to think," the voice interrupted. "You were brought in because we need to see results. I'm not seeing very many results today."

"We are doing everything we can to stall her efforts, but

she somehow continues to press forward. Having her arrested seemed to be a stroke of genius, but her incarceration didn't last nearly as long as we thought it would."

"GET IT DONE!" boomed the voice on the other end. "I don't need your sniveling, and I don't want your excuses. Do your job, and if you can't I'll have no other choice but to have you replaced. And that is a proposition you certainly do not want us to entertain."

"Yes. We will get the job done."

"Good!" The line went dead.

Tuesday, September 17th – 11:00 p.m
Donatella Residence (300 Calgary Lane)

Agent Donatella Dabria sat on the edge of her bed in her tan silk two-piece pajama set with an old shoe box across her lap. Four 6x9 glossy photos from her past were spread over the bed. She picked up the first photo, a picture of her parents on their seventh anniversary. Her mom had been captured in a hearty laugh as her dad was whispering in her ear. She always wondered what her dad had said to her mom to elicit such a reaction. She held onto this picture because it captured in that one instance the love they shared with one another.

The second picture was from her college graduation. In this picture, though she was smiling, she could remember the feelings she had on this day. For many this was the happiest day of their lives, but for Donatella it was a moment of indescribable pain. She was reminded of losing her parents and the fact they would never have the opportunity to see her graduate and start her life. She remembered going to her car after the ceremony crying and holding herself. For ten minutes she cried and then she started her car, already packed with her belongings and ready to leave the campus.

The third picture was of her and her fellow bureau recruits outside of the training facility on a rainy day. She recalled the constant barrage they had taken that day, and for every blow the instructors dished out she stood back up pushing for more. The group, haggard in the photo, never gave up and neither would she.

The fourth photo was Donatella holding a baby.

"Donatella, you have to hurry. I'm not sure if I can hold it any longer."

"Liz, I'm pushing the car as fast as I can, plus getting you and the baby there safely is the first priority. And of all times for Frank to be out of town for work, today had to be the day."

"Well if you don't push this car any harder, the baby will be born right here on the side of the road!"

"I hear you, Liz. You focus on the breathing and holding that baby in and I'll focus on the traffic and getting us to the hospital."

"She seems to have a mind of her own. Breathing isn't stopping – Oh God, there is another one! Damn it, Donatella, she is coming, hurry!"

"Liz, I see the hospital right around the corner. Stay strong. We're almost there."

"Stay strong – Ha! Coming from the woman who doesn't have an eight-pound bowling ball rearranging her organs trying to make entry into this world.

Donatella recalled how they barely made it to the

hospital. Once they arrived, the nurses took Liz immediately up to the delivery room and two hours later Bree Elizabeth Hartley was born. Liz, probably in baby-induced stress, asked Donatella if she would be Bree's Godmother. Donatella immediately said yes. This was one of the biggest honors for Donatella, one she didn't plan to take lightly.

At this moment I'm failing you, Bree. Someone has you, and I know you are scared. Out loud she stated, "I'll find you soon enough, Bree, and whoever did this will pay!"

Tuesday, September 17th – 11:00 p.m
Dresser Household (1135 Milton Court)

DIANE DRESSER PACED the wooden floor of the family room while her husband was stowed away in his study talking on the phone with the door closed. She too was burning to make a call, but she didn't know if this was too soon. Finally, everything she had wanted was looking as if it could, as if it would, come true.

The affair with Douglas Grant had been going on for years. But he refused to leave his wife and their child. *What a joke*, she thought. *That boy was no more his son than he was mine.* The fact Thomas Grant was really Bill's son originally infuriated her, but then she realized this was the grounds for divorce she had been looking for since the affair started. She could probably take Bill to the cleaners while she was at it. In reality, she didn't need the money. She had grown up a trust-fund baby and had never worked a day in her life, while Bill worked hard to earn his fortune. A fortune, that for spite and no other reason, she would see end up in her bank account when this loveless marriage had ended.

When they were first married, she loved Bill. He had rugged good looks, was the CEO of his own software company, and was on top of the world. She met him at a speed-dating event in Uptown Charlotte and was ready to dismiss him. But there was something about him that she just couldn't let go. When it was time to change partners, she asked him to stay a little longer, so he did. They exchanged numbers and met a few times for drinks and dinner. Before she knew it, they were making passionate love in the back of her Mercedes E 450. No doubt the sex was amazing, but this was where things changed.

For Diane, it was all about the sex and the secret rendezvous. For Bill, he seemed to be falling in love. When Bill asked her to marry him a year later, she was torn. On one hand she was having fun, but she wasn't sure she was ready to settle down. On the other hand, her parents had a long-lasting marriage, so she figured it couldn't be all bad. He had gone all out with the band playing her favorite song, at least the song he thought was her favorite that in reality she really despised. He had flown her family in as a surprise to witness what he knew would be a yes to his question. Bill wanted them to witness the moment first-hand, and he wanted them to be part of the festivities. With her family awaiting her decision with bated breath, the unyielding pressure mounting, she said yes.

And once again the excitement was back. Planning for the wedding was exhilarating. The dress fitting where she tried on every dress she wanted, and though she was only going to buy the one she felt like a queen for the five days it took to pick. Picking the venue was one of her favorite tasks on the checklist. She wanted to pick a venue that made her the talk of the town for many years to come, because this was going to be her day. And it was. She was a stunningly beautiful bride and a sight to behold.

However, by the time they were reaching their first anniversary, she realized how much of a mistake she'd made. She carried on as best she could for another year and then decided she was through pretending. But she didn't know of an easy way out.

Later that year Bill introduced her to Douglas and Sylvia Grant. Bill had lent Douglas some of his R&D team to complete the design and development of the new AI chip that would be used as part of the new virtual reality system Douglas was designing. Diane, always up for a challenge, wondered if she could seduce Douglas into bed. She could see how devoted he was to his wife and thus this was what made the challenge worthwhile.

It took nearly six months, but finally he broke, like she knew he would. It was a rainy day and she was just making her way back home from the Whole Foods market. As she was pulling into the driveway, she noticed Douglas's car and him standing at the door. She of course knew Bill wasn't home, and she didn't know the reason for Douglas's visit. As it turned out, he was bringing by the latest prototype of the VR system that he wanted Bill to try as soon as possible. Diane suggested that he could bring the prototype into the house and leave it in Bill's study so he could review it once he arrived home.

Douglas grabbed the box from the back of his trunk and walked into the house. He had been to their house enough times at this point that he knew his way to the study. Diane was determined she would not miss this opportunity. She unclasped her bra, pulled it from beneath her white blouse and tossed the garment into one of the grocery bags. She then slowly walked to the mailbox at the end of the driveway, soaking in every raindrop that hit her shirt. She then made her way through the garage, through the kitchen, down the foyer and into the study. Douglas was just about to exit the room when he caught an eyeful of the skin plastered underneath Diane's soaked shirt. While his brain tried to find an escape route, Diane pressed her advantage by literally pressing her body into his. As he opened his mouth to protest, she caught his words with her lips, and then her tongue as she kissed him deeply, and he kissed her back.

They made love right there in the study and countless other times after that night. For Diane, what started off as a way to add excitement into her life, turned into something she had never dreamed. She had truly fallen in love with this man. Maybe it was the thrill of the chase and the conquest that did it for her, but unlike with Bill she felt a tangible spark every time they were together. A spark that she had not once felt with Bill and thus solidified in her mind that their marriage needed to end, but how to do this was the question.

Blinking her eyes back to the here and now, Diane had made up her mind. She opened up the contact list of her phone to call Douglas. She would tell him that even though he had lost his son, well a boy who in reality was not his son, it was time for him to leave his wife. He could use the fact she was unfaithful, birthed a child that did not belong to him, and lied to him for over a decade about the paternity of the kid as the reason for the divorce. She loved him, and it was time for them to start their life together.

She found the number she was in search of and touched the green phone receiver icon to begin the transmission.

One ring, two rings.

She was getting more and more excited about the future they would start together.

Three rings.

They would probably need to leave this community, and she was okay with that. She didn't much care for the neighbors if she was being honest with herself.

Four rings.

She began to wonder if they would have any children. There had been advancements in technology and though she and Bill were told she could not have children, that was ages ago. She would need to schedule an appointment with her OB to discuss options. She could already see herself having a baby with Doug.

Voicemail

Diane eyed the phone incredulously as if voicemail was foreign to her, which of course it was not. But never before had Douglas ignored her call.

"You have reached the voicemail of Douglas Grant. Unfortunately, I cannot come to the phone right now, but if you would leave your name and number, I will return your call at my earliest convenience."

Beep

"Your earliest convenience!" Diane raged. "You do not let my phone calls go to voicemail. You answer them, damn it!" Diane mashed the red receiver icon on the touchscreen with as much ferocity as she could muster to end the call. She missed the days when she could slam down a receiver.

To make herself feel better, she hurled the phone across the room, shattering the device into several pieces.

Wednesday, September 18th – 11:00 a.m
Donatella Residence (300 Calgary Lane)

DONATELLA SAT in the two-story library within her chateau, carefully considering what she knew about the case and what she suspected to be true. She knew the death of Thomas Grant was done to send a message to the Hartley's. Donatella knew this because she received correspondence from Elizabeth shortly after the breaking news.

"They have Bree. Communication compromised," came the hurried message from Liz.

She knew someone was feeding information to the reporter, Sal Grandson, to purposely obfuscate the truth. The disappearance of Thomas Grant was mere window dressing. Similar to a magician who will have your eyes focused to the right while performing the root of the trick to the left. Whoever it was, they were controlling the narrative, and hopefully after her discussion with Grandson that avenue would now be closed to them.

She knew someone planned for her to be arrested in order to abduct Bree. Donatella didn't believe in coincidences, and for Bree's kidnapping to be timed with her arrest she was sure of this fact. What she didn't know was how they managed to have the police move so fast.

She suspected that someone in the neighborhood had something to do with the disappearance of both children. There wasn't any hard proof to substantiate this belief, but both kidnappings were too clean. These were bright children, and they would not go somewhere willingly with someone they didn't know. There didn't seem to be a sign of any struggle, therefore she didn't believe either child was drugged and then taken away. Many of the children in the neighborhood knew one another, so odds are they would feel safe with anyone else in the neighborhood.

Yet, Bree was the outlier. She was new to the neighborhood and knew the stakes they were playing. She would not have trusted anyone in the neighborhood. In fact, Bree would not have trusted anyone at all. And this was what perplexed Agent Dabria. Bree would have been hypersensitive to her surroundings, and for there to be no physical evidence to her disappearance didn't compute for Donatella.

She also suspected that the window dressing was not complete.

Thursday, September 19th – 7:30 p.m
Driftwood Springs Open Field

"Come on guys, one more game. Donny, you know you want revenge for the way I beat you on the deep post to score the game-winning touchdown."

"Jeffery, I can't. We've already played two more games than we probably should have. The sun will be setting completely in the next few minutes, and with everything happening around here lately my mom doesn't want me out after dark."

I still have my daddy's shotgun, Jeffery thought but

decided not to press the issue. As the group parted to take their various paths home, Jeffery decided he should do the same; home was the last place he wanted to be at this moment.

For tonight was Thursday night, the night his father went out with his friends from high school. Many of which were unmarried, living the bachelor life. On several occasions after going out with his friends, Jeffery's father had come home completely loaded, wasted, angry.

Early this year, on March 14th, Jeffery had experienced one of the scariest moments from his father. He could recall the day for two reasons. First, it was the night he scored his first ever winning goal in their soccer match. He was the right-winger for the game and had streaked down the sideline pounding as hard as he could to catch up with the ball that had been lobbed over the defense by their midfielder. He could feel his heart racing as he realized he would catch up to the ball, and the only person between him and glory was Thomas Grant. He caught up with the ball outside of the penalty box and began his dribble toward the goal. He pressed his advantaged by angling toward the left post in an effort to get Thomas moving, and he did just as Jeffery expected.

Jeffery had dissected Thomas's game before and realized if he could get him moving in one direction and suddenly pivot and change directions, he had the advantage. Thomas was a good goalie, for the most part, but had not mastered the change in directions.

Jeffery dribbled feverishly. Right to left, left to right, right to left, left to right all the while keeping his angle toward the left post. He wanted to have Thomas fixated on his rhythm so that he could make his move.

Right to left, left to right, it was almost time to strike. Jeffery could see Thomas leaning ever so slowly and knew it was time. He made the pass one more time from his right foot to his left foot, and as quick as an attacking cobra Jeffery kicked the ball with his left foot toward the right post. A flicker of dismay in his eyes betrayed Thomas's normally cool demeanor.

Thomas scurried to recover while the ball was traveling nearly 65 miles per hour toward the net. He reached up with his left hand in an effort to deflect the shot, but it was too late. The ball flew nearly a foot above his outstretching hand and cradled securely in the back of the net.

Jeffery threw his hands into the air in exultation while Thomas pounded the ground with his fist in pure frustration. Peering over toward the crowd, Jeffery saw his mom standing and giving the fans in her section a series of high fives in between her wild clapping and cheering.

Making their way home, Jeffery told his mother he couldn't wait to tell his dad about his game winning goal, which lead to the second reason Jeffery could recall the date with clarity.

Jeffery's mom agreed that he could tell his father about his game winning goal if he was awake when he arrived. In his excitement, Jeffery was too keyed up to sleep. Jeffery heard the motor on the garage door start up and sensed the movement of the door as it began to lift. His father was home, and Jeffery was bursting with excitement. A few moments later, he heard the chime from the door disengaging from the door jamb followed by his mother greeting his father.

He hopped out of the bed, feet hitting the throw rug on

his wooden bedroom floor, and began making his way down the stairs. Halfway down he heard a loud sound of a hand smacking against flesh and heard his mother bellow out a yell. The sound froze him in his steps.

"I could have had everything," his father slurred as he advanced on his wife, who sprawled along the bottom of the steps. "You trapped me!" he said, bending at the waist and pulling Mrs. Carter like a rag doll to her feet. "You got pregnant and everything changed." He raised his voice and pulled his wife to her tip toes, so she was eye to eye with him. "Everything changed!"

He glared at Mrs. Carter as if he meant to strike her again. With the veins pulsating wildly behind his blood shot eyes, he said, "I despise what you have done to me!" He spoke this while dumping his wife back onto the floor. She folded into herself as Jeffery's dad, Alton Carter, turned to walk out of the door. At which time, Jeffery noticed the wording on the back of his father's shirt. "St. Patrick's Day Weekend Kickoff Mar 14 – Mar 17, 2019." And the bottom of the shirt read, "Riverdale High 20th Class Reunion."

On a minimum of once a month, always on a Thursday, after spending time with his high school friends, Jeffery's father would come home in a rage and take it out on Jeffery's mom. It had not yet happened this month, and Jeffery feared that tonight would be the night. Tonight, would be the night Alton Carter would come home and put his hands on Jeffery's mother, and Jeffery didn't want to be there to witness it. Many times Jeffery thought about standing up to his dad, defending his mother. But to date he had not. He had not stood up to his father because he didn't know how and didn't know if he could.

Jeffery continued to meander through the streets,

dreading the moment he would arrive at his house. He was shaking with fright, concerned with what he would see when he walked through the door. Would he hear the sobs of his mother cascading down the stairs as she trembled from behind their bedroom door? Or worse, would he walk in on the abuse as it was happening real-time? Deciding the later could be true, he decided to take a detour to lengthen the amount of time it would take for him to arrive home.

Making a left-hand turn on Rose Street, Jeffery was met with a car idling on the corner with the light off. Panic and self-preservation were two emotions that had not registered in the young lad's mind, and that lapse of awareness would be his downfall.

10

THURSDAY, SEPTEMBER 19TH – 7:40 P.M
DRIFTWOOD SPRINGS NEIGHBORHOOD

Jeffery approached the black sedan with the nonchalance of a child running through a grassy field on a hot summer day. He casually looked through the rear window only to find the window was tinted, a deep smoke color thwarting his attempt to look inside. Passing the rear bumper, he could see that the driver's side window, though tinted, was not as dark as the rear view window. Coolly he turned his head as he inched closer to the driver's side window to take a better peek. To his disbelief, the seat was empty. *I wonder where they could be?*

Just then a hand reached over his shoulder, clamping over his mouth, pulling him backward. Jeffery screamed, but his voice was muted by the black leather glove now starving his brain of the oxygen he needed. Jeffery reached back in an attempt to grab anything on this assailant that he could, but there wasn't anything he could grasp. *He's got me! Momma help me! He's got me!* Jeffery thought in frantic gasps. He tried to drop to his butt to throw his attacker off balance, but all of his 110 lb. frame was supported by the strength of the attacker suspending Jeffery in midair. He began to kick wildly while being pulled backward, left shoe flying ahead of him and landing ten feet in the middle of the road. Jeffery, mind racing and eyes darting, couldn't seem to find a solution to his problem. He knew without a shadow of a doubt if he didn't do something he could end up like Thomas. He didn't want to die; he didn't want to have his mother morn his loss like Mrs. Grant was morning the loss of her son.

He heard the latch of the trunk disengage and knew he only had moments left. He screamed again. And again, it came out as a faint whisper. *This is it. I'm not going to make it*!

Suddenly, Jeffery, the car, the kidnapper, were all flooded with a bright light. One that could only be coming from that of a police car. Jeffery was dropped to the ground, head hitting the concrete as the trunk slammed shut. He next heard the sound of the car dropping into gear and then speeding off.

The approaching car stopped next to the fallen boy. The driver of the car made his way over to Jeffery. "Are you okay, son?"

Jeffery looked up to the officer to find it was Detective Wilson. "Yes, sir. Thank you! Thank you!" he said, dropping his head to the chest of the detective, tears flowing down his cheeks.

"You're safe, son," Wilson said, helping the young man to his feet. "I have already placed a call with the dispatcher. All patrol cars will be on the lookout for the vehicle and the person who did this to you. We will find him."

Detective Wilson opened the front door of the car ushering Jeffery inside. "Sit here. I'll get you to your parents' house." Moments earlier getting to his parents' house was the last thing Jeffery wanted, but now that was the only place he wanted to be. Detective Wilson climbed into the driver's seat and began to make his way toward the Carter's house. As they were moving forward, Jeffery heard what he thought was a thud from behind him. He quickly looked back and didn't see anything. Remembering he dislodged his foot from his shoe that likely ended up in the middle of the road, he figured this was likely the source of the sound. However, later this would turn out to be an untrue rationalization.

Thursday, September 19th – 8:45 p.m:
Grandson Residence (4208 Jasper Road)

SAL STILL HAD NOT RECOVERED from his encounter on Tuesday the 17th with Special Agent Dabria. During his time in New York, he had gone toe to toe with his share of shady individuals. He had even done so with individuals he believed were part of some mob families, though nothing was ever proven. However, the intensity of her glare, those hazelnut eyes piercing his soul, the manner in which she carried herself. That was the first time Sal ever had a bead of sweat trickle down the center of his back tracing his spine until it dissipated on his well-worn Jockey boxer briefs.

"What does she mean I need to give her a call should I hear anything further? Why should I hear anything at all? It's not like I'm the killer's personal secretary." He pondered this thought out loud to no one in particular.

But inside his journalist heart, he knew she was right. For some unknown reason someone involved with this case had sought him out as a conduit to spread news of the case. He didn't want to look a gift horse in the mouth since he was getting a first-hand account of the story of his lifetime. But he felt a sense of unease because two kids had disappeared, one of which had already turned up dead. He feared this would not be the end, not by a long shot.

"I might as well move my weary bones from this sofa and get to work," he said to no one in particular. Living alone for a number of years had created a habit in Sal that most people would not have figured. He talked out loud to himself on a regular basis. Very rarely in the presence of others, yet nearly all the time when he was at home. He felt this helped him to reason out the dilemmas he had in front of him, and as his mother always said, "As long as you don't start answering yourself, you aren't crazy." Sal loved that crazy old bird.

Plopping down in the beat-up kitchen table chair missing half of the wood back support, Sal fired up his computer. While he waited on the computer to come to life, he began to ponder his next article.

"There is more to this story than what I'm being led to believe, but exactly what am I missing? Thomas and Bree have no connection from what I've been able to uncover, but the kidnapper, the killer, went after these two children for a reason." On the top of his 5x7 yellow flip tablet, he removed the top sheet exposing a fresh piece of paper. At the top of the paper he scrawled, "Why these two?" He placed his well-chewed pen in the corner of his mouth and bit down. Staring at the paper, he crossed out, "Why these two?" and beneath that he wrote, "Possible decoy?" He underlined this question three times and placed the pen on his tablet.

His computer had come to life, and he clicked on the email icon. He had three new emails. The first one was a junk email advising him to change his car insurance. The second was a confirmation email from Amazon that his Technic Porsche Lego set had been shipped and would arrive tomorrow. He was looking forward to having down time to put that together. Then came the third email.

"Now this is a surprise." He said aloud with a smirk on his face. It was an email from Jane Markowitz. The subject line read, "In town." This piqued his interest. He picked up the pen, placed it back into his mouth, and bit down hard. He stared at the subject line for what seemed like a minute, but in reality, was ten seconds.

"What game are you playing, Jane?" Knowing the only way he would receive an answer would be to open the email. He positioned the mouse over the subject ready to tap the message so that the preview would appear on screen. Just as he prepared to click, another message appeared.

From: Anonymous

Subject: Driftwood Springs – Another child missing

Forgoing the desire to open the email from Jane, he blew the pen from his mouth allowing it to fall to the table and opened the new message. Upon opening the email, he saw the message was short and had only two sentences.

"Another child has been kidnapped. Have you looked into Douglas Grant?"

"A third child? Have I looked into Douglas Grant? Is this anonymous person trying to tell me that Douglas Grant had something to do with his son's disappearance, the disappearance of Bree Singleton, and now this third child? What would be Douglas's motive? No, he couldn't be involved. His own son is now dead."

Sal laid his head back on the top of the wooden chair. Blindly he reached across the tabletop until he found his pen and placed the chewed end back in his mouth. He closed his eyes and saw the words from the email appear in stark white lettering in the darkness behind his closed eyelids.

"Another child has been kidnapped. Have you looked into Douglas Grant?"

"I need to call Special Agent Dabria." He opened his eyes and looked down at the two words he wrote on his tablet, "Possible decoy?" He took the pen from his mouth and circled the words until they were surrounded in a dark black halo. He then picked up his phone and dialed the number for Agent Dabria.

Thursday, September 19th – 8:30 p.m
Donatella Residence (300 Calgary Lane)

DONATELLA WALKED UP to the path leading to her front door. She was returning from her walk past the Hartley's home. She knew she would not enter the residence, but she at least wanted to view it from the outside to ensure things looked okay. Reaching the front door, she entered her six-digit number on the keypad to unlock the door. Hearing the deadbolt disengage, she pressed down on the handle and began to swing the door open. All too late she faintly heard the sound of quickening footsteps behind her.

Donatella felt a searing pain punch the middle of her back, forcing her headfirst into the door. The impact forced the door open fully, and she slid face first across the floor. The attacker was on her quickly, taking no time to close the door. She was yanked from the floor with a pair of strong, masculine hands. Quickly cycling through her training, she knew she needed to get back to her base, face her attacker, and determine her mode of attack. However, her first movement needed to be that of self-defense.

She felt her attacker preparing to slam her back to the floor, *more brawn than finesse.* She shot both feet back aiming for the kneecaps, but this man was taller than she expected, and she kicked him in both shins. Though the heels of her feet missed the target by mere inches, the blow resulted in the assailant dropping her to the floor instead of forcing her through the floor. Like a cat, Donatella was able to leap back to her feet while simultaneously performing a 180 degree turn to face her attacker.

The motion sensor light in the foyer that activated when she came tumbling through the door gave her a good look at this man –this beast. As she surmised, he was big. 6 foot 4 big with meat cleaver paws as hands. His head sat upon a tree trunk neck that melded into his ever-expanding shoulders. His torso, disproportion to the lower half of his body, was draped with tattoos that she could see pulsating underneath his white, nearly transparent, performance muscle shirt. Donatella wondered with amazement how a man this size was able to move with such stealth.

This beast-man tilted his head methodically to the left, cracking the muscles holding up his head, and then again to the right, giving an audible satisfying sigh. With speed that did not match his girth, he bolted towards Donatella, who in turn deftly chopped him in the throat with her right hand. A method that normally worked didn't faze this man one bit as he snatched her departing hand from his neck. Donatella, in attack mode for the moment, kneed him twice in succession to his ribs. She could see looking into his eyes as he wrenched her hand backward that the first blow had no effect, but the second caused a slight grimace. Balancing quickly, she flipped into the direction he was wrenching her arm as he was attempting to snap the bone.

She landed on one knee while bringing his arm down with her a few inches. His grip loosened to the point her hand was now caught within his grasp. Not wasting any time, she brought her left hand over to her right, clasping his hand between hers. Though his hands were bigger, she understood leverage. With all the strength she could muster, she grabbed the pointer and middle finger just above the joint, yanked and heard the loud snap of the two fingers disjointing as she pulled back on them. The man howled in pain, her right hand fell free, and she was back on her feet.

Sizing up this opponent, she needed to quickly analyze him for any weakness she could exploit. She noticed out of the corner of her right eye a glint of metal aiming directly for her neck. Reflexively she raised her left shoulder in defense and was greeted with the burning sensation of metal piercing skin. *Where in the hell did that knife come from?*

She needed to end this fight fast before she would be unable to come out on top. She reached over to the table, grabbed the vase filled with Blue Ocean Breeze Orchids, and smashed the vase across the left side of his head. The blow didn't cause the vase to shatter, but it did cause this giant to stumble to his right. Not waiting for him to regain his footing, she turned the vase upside down, spilling the water and the orchids onto the floor. She grabbed the neck of the vase with both hands, pulled it back behind her neck and swung with all of her might. The glass crumbled into shards, cutting her in several locations on both hands. She noticed the giant tilting forward. Pressing her advantage, she pulled his neck closer to the ground while simultaneously lifting her left knee to meet his left ribs. This maneuver stung her left shoulder, which was now pouring with blood.

She kneed the same rib, once, twice, three more times until she heard the crunch of one or more breaking. While she hoped the broken rib or ribs wouldn't puncture his heart, if it did, she wouldn't give a damn. It would be one less scumbag on this planet. Her assailant was now fully bent over at the waist, gasping for air, but he was still on his feet. Donatella did a ninety-degree turn to her left, jumped into the air, and brought her elbow down on the base of his neck; he tumbled face down on the floor while she landed halfway on him. She rolled over on her back, laying in the water with Orchids sprawled out across the floor.

Thursday, September 19th – 8:30 p.m
Driftwood Springs Neighborhood

JASMYN ABSOLUTELY LOVED THE FALL. Of the four seasons, fall was by far her favorite. The leaves began to change colors, the temperature began to cool day by day, and it meant it was time for chili and crock pot cooking. She picked up a new Instant Pot a few weeks ago, and she couldn't wait to try out some new recipes. Fall also meant light sweaters and walks with their dog, Maggie, when the sun went down. The couple typically shared these duties and, on several occasions, would take the jaunt together, but Marcellous had inspiration strike for a passage in his next novel and decided to stay behind to spill his words onto the page. So, for tonight, it was just the girls, and for Jasmyn this was okay. This walk would give her some time to clear her head and think about the news she needed to give Marcellous. Her period was late, which had happened before, but it was never this late. So, this morning she had taken a pregnancy test and it confirmed her feminine intuition, *I'm pregnant.*

The couple talked about having a baby and decided they would try, so she had come off of the pill. This was four months ago, and each month was met with another moment of disappointment. But now she was pregnant and so excited, but she wasn't sure how to tell Marcellous. She wanted to perform some great and magical reveal for him, but she felt guilty knowing that the Grants had just heard the news that their son had been murdered. And with the disappearances happening in the neighborhood, it just didn't feel right.

She had stewed over this dilemma all day and finally decided she would simply tell him. They would hug, cry, probably hug again, and he would probably ask did that mean they couldn't have sex anymore. She smiled at this thought, and she loved him with all of her heart. Just as she prepared to tell him, his inspiration struck, and he moved into the den to write. She waited ten minutes, twenty minutes, and finally after twenty-seven minutes she decided she would take Maggie for a walk. Maybe this was the Lord letting her know this was not the best way to tell him the news.

"Well Lord, you have me out here walking up and down the street. I need you to give me an answer or a sign of some sort. I clearly shouldn't withhold this information from Marcellous, right?" she asked, looking up to the star filled sky. She felt the slack in Maggie's collar go taut and said, "What's wrong girl?" Maggie didn't respond verbally but did her best to pull the holder of her leash forward. Sensing Maggie's urgency, Jasmyn began to move more swiftly.

"What's got you so wound up?" she asked again and again receiving only the response of urgency in the step of her dog, now in a mild trot. Maggie was headed for the house of Donatella Bianchi.

"Maggie, no! Stop!"

Maggie did just that and sat at the end of the driveway staring up toward the door. Jasmyn's eyes trailed the outline of the driveway until she glanced the front door. From her viewpoint she could see that the front door was ajar.

"Is that what has you so keyed up, Maggie? People leave their doors open sometimes. That doesn't mean –"

She heard a yell from within the house. The yell sounded like that of a man. Jasmyn looked down at Maggie, who by now was springing into action. She pulled Jasmyn forward as she was not expecting this move from her retriever, now in a full sprint. Jasmyn, thinking *this is a bad idea,* ran with the dog as she didn't want to be pulled off of her feet and potentially harm the new life she was carrying around inside of her body.

She heard a muffled thud followed by what sounded like a splash of water hitting the ground. Three seconds later she heard the indistinguishable sound of glass breaking. Maggie gagged slightly at the collar tight around her neck as she pulled Jasmyn forward, continuing to push forward regardless of the pain she was feeling. Jasmyn turned her feet over faster so that she could catch up to her dog.

She heard a second thud shortly followed by a third lighter thud. By this time, she was at the doorway. She witnessed a man lying face down on the ground just as Donatella was rolling over onto some blue Orchids. However, Donatella didn't stop with the roll onto her back, she completed the roll with one fluid motion, pulled a gun from beneath the table next to her and pointed the barrel at Jasmyn.

"Don't shoot!" she exclaimed as Maggie echoed with two barks. "It's Jasmyn Thompson!" she blurted out while quickly lifting her hands. She wasn't sure why she said her name, but it may have just saved her life.

"What are you doing here, Mrs. Thompson?" Donatella asked in a slightly ragged voice.

"I heard commotion and came running. Is he dead? What happened here"

"I think he may be unconscious." She looked over and noticed the slight movements of a man breathing but not moving. "He attacked me as I walked in through the front door." She favored her left shoulder as she sat up.

"Oh my God, you're bleeding!" Jasmyn dropped the leash, ran into the house, and her years training as a nurse took over. She quickly surveyed the foyer, looking for anything to stop the flow of blood, quickly taking in how gorgeous the house was on the inside. This was her first time in Donatella's house and she loved it.

"Do you have any towels?"

"Down the foyer, make a left at the end. You'll run into the downstairs suite. You can find a towel in the bathroom."

Jasmyn ran past the prostate form laid across the floor and headed for the back room. Maggie made her way next to Donatella, who was now sitting fully erect, examining her shoulder. She turned and looked at the retriever with those beautiful puppy-like brown eyes. Donatella reached out and rubbed the dog on the back of the head, behind the right ear. Maggie laid her head on Donatella's lap as Jasmyn made her way back from the bathroom.

She returned with a couple of towels and a first aid kit. "Here, let me take a look at that." Jasmyn pulled a pair of scissors from the kit and cut away the fabric around Donatella's shoulder. She separated one of the towels and began to clear away the blood so she could take a closer look. Though there was a lot of blood, from what Jasmyn could see there wasn't a severe injury. She reached into the kit from some disinfectant and poured this directly to the wound. Donatella winced, but no sound emanated from her vocals.

"You're going to need stitches. What I have in this kit can do a quick and crude job, but you should be seen by the ER."

"Go ahead and do what you can do," Donatella said flatly.

Jasmyn looked at Donatella, wanting to say more but decided to hold her tongue. She reached into the kit and found what she needed to start the stitching process. As Jasmyn began prepping the wound, Donatella reached down into her right front jean pocket and retrieved a vibrating cell phone.

Donatella looked at the caller ID and realized the call was coming in from Sal Grandson. "Yes, Sal."

"I received another email, another kid has been kidnapped"

"Damn it. I'll be there shortly!"

She disconnected the line and looked over to Jasmyn. "When you are done, I need you to drive me to Sal's. Bring the pup."

Jasmyn was taken aback. *Was that a question, a demand, or both?* The matter of fact way in which Donatella made the statement came across as almost authoritative. "Sure," was the first thing she could say. "What about him?" she said, nodding over to the massive man on the floor.

"I have someone who can come take care of that. With haste now if you would, Mrs. Thompson."

Thursday, September 19th – 9:15 p.m
Grandson Residence (4208 Jasper Road)

THIRTY MINUTES after placing the call to SA Dabria, Sal heard a knock at his door. Quickly he rose to his feet and traversed the hallway, anticipating the discussion he and the special agent would have regarding this latest disappearance. He was also considering disclosing his hunch about a possible decoy.

Swinging the door open, Sal's eyes first bulged, followed shortly by a double take, then an immediate step back. Agent

Dabria stood before him with hands bandaged as if she were interrupted during mummy preparation. She favored her left shoulder, which was encased in a hastily thrown together sling made from shreds of cloth. She stood with a slight slouch and not the erect gracefulness he had seen in her previously.

Sal's double-take response stemmed from the stark beauty who stood next to the beleaguered special agent, a woman he had never seen before. Although she was in a pair of sweatpants and a simple cotton spun t-shirt, this other woman was radiant. His reverie was short-lived as he looked down at the dog sitting patiently but alert enough to spring into action if the need arose.

Sal recovered quickly but not gracefully, "My Lord, what happened to you? I mean, come in. Can I get you some water, whiskey, both?"

"No," Agent Dabria stated, walking past him with a shortened, limping gate. "This is Jasmyn Thompson, a neighbor from the subdivision, her dog Maggie. What do you have Sal?"

Prepared for this question, he walked the trio over to his laptop that still sat on his kitchen table. Sal took his seat in the familiar wooden chair, picked up his chewed pen, placed it into his mouth, and typed in his password. The screen came to life as the hum from the laptop's fan increased with the new visual strain. Agent Dabria and Jasmyn looked over Sal's shoulder at the two sentences that were displayed on the screen.

"Another child has been kidnapped. Have you looked into Douglas Grant?"

"There it is. The latest email I received from this person, or group, Anonymous. When you were leaving your community, did you notice any activity that could support this claim?"

Donatella thought back to their departure from the subdivision and realized she hadn't noticed much of anything. Her keen sense of awareness had once again failed her, and this was something she would need to resolve with intense meditation. In an answer to the question posed by Sal, she flatly responded, "No."

"Yeah, strange. No activity in the neighborhood and a definitive assertion that this has happened. Whoever we are dealing with has insider information. What do you make of the second sentence? 'Have you looked into Douglas Grant?'" He decided he would lob his thought into the atmosphere to see how it was received.

"I'm starting to believe there is a decoy of some sort with these disappearances. The first two victims don't seem to have any connection other than they went to the same school and lived in the same subdivision. For Thomas Grant to be found at the construction site being run by his father's company already struck me as odd. And when I received this email, I became more convinced that someone was trying to point us toward Douglas Grant while concealing their true motive. I mean, come on. First, why would Douglas Grant kill his own son, and "B" why would he leave the body of his son at a location that points directly back to him. This makes no sense."

Jasmyn chuckled silently to herself with Sal's First and "B" linear connections.

Agent Dabria had a separate train of thought. She was 100% confident that the ploy was to mask the disappearance of Bree in with these other kidnapping, if indeed it turned out that another child was missing. But Sal made a connection that he was not yet aware he had made.

Thomas Grant was not the child of Douglas Grant, and Bree Singleton was really Bree Hartley. That in itself was the connection. Both children had a secret that no one else was aware of, yet obviously someone knew this connection. How could she have missed this before?

Agent Dabria pulled out her cell phone and dialed a number. After three rings, the voice of Bryce Jacobs permeated through the handset. Jacobs, who went by "BJ," was a child genius. At the age of fifteen he scored a perfect score on the ACT, 36 out of 36, followed up the next week with a perfect score on the SAT, 1600 out of 1600. BJ spent most of his academic youth in fruitless fights with his instructors, as he felt he knew more than they could offer. Finally, at the age of fifteen, with perfect scores on both the ACT and the SAT, he petitioned to be accepted into MIT though he had not received his high school diploma. He won his petition, enrolled that same fall and within two years he graduated Summa Cum Laude and sat at the top of his class.

At eighteen, he had graduated from the top technology school in the country and concluded his fight with the academic system. However, he hadn't planned for what was next. Bored out of his mind, he decided he would write an algorithm that would predict the outcome of the lottery. Many people had used mathematical formulas before to predict where the scratch off tickets would land, but no one had truly succeeded in predicting the lottery numbers.

BJ focused his initial efforts in his hometown of Chicago, IL. The winning numbers obtained by normal and legal means could be pulled from the lottery's website. However, the data only went back one year. He knew he would need more data for his statistical analysis, so he broke into the lottery database and was able to retrieve twenty-five years of lottery data. Within three months he was able to correctly predict the Pick-3 95% of the time, the Pick-4, 80% of the time, and the Lotto 55% of the time.

He popped up on the FBI radar when he accessed the lottery databases in four other states, Ohio, Virginia, Tennessee, and North Carolina. Agent Dabria was put in charge of the case, and she worked meticulously to collar this criminal. However, he would not face any jail time. Although he had accessed the databases illegally across multiple states, he did not profit from his efforts. He had not played the lottery, and he had not capitalized on this algorithm he created. He was put on five years' probation at the request of Agent Dabria and the two stayed in constant contact over the years.

Every so often Agent Dabria would reach out to BJ when she needed something done that she felt toed the ethical line, figured no one else could do, or simply because she also didn't like to follow the rules.

BJ spoke with a calm, measured diction that gave the air of confidence. "Special Agent Dabria, what a pleasure to hear from you. It's been far too long. As much as I would like to catch up, I'm sure this is not a social call. What can I do for you?"

"Bryce –"

"BJ, if you wouldn't mind."

"Fine, BJ, I need you to trace the origins of an email that was sent to a colleague."

"A lover type colleague?" BJ asked.

Ignoring the comment, Agent Dabria continued without missing stride. "The email was sent to Sal Grandson, and he received this email roughly forty-five minutes ago." She gave BJ the additional information he requested in order to complete the trace.

"This should be a simple matter. Is there anything else I can do for you at this moment?"

"No. Please hurry."

"I will. No need to be pushy!"

Agent Dabria disconnected the phone. When she did, she noticed Sal giving her a questioning glare.

"You never did answer my question when you arrived. What happened to you?" By this time the four of them, Sal, Agent Dabria, Jasmyn, and Maggie had moved into the cramped living room. Agent Dabria crossed her left leg over her right. "I was attacked entering my home by an unknown assailant."

"At your home!" Sal said incredulously. "How in the hell could something like this happen? I was envious of Dale and Carmen when they moved into the "gated community" at Driftwood Springs with the gorgeous houses and plush living. However, on my salary as a journalist affording to live there is nearly impossible. Everyone there must have some great inheritance or they work at a stellar job. And to be honest, for it to be a gated community, the last few days have seen some serious crime. It's like they will let anyone in regardless of who they are."

Agent Dabria replayed the words from Sal. *Everyone there must have some great inheritance, or they work at a stellar job. They will let anyone in regardless of who they are.* A concrete thought began to crystallize in her mind. "Sal, do you mind if I use your bathroom?"

"Sure. Second door on the right."

Great inheritance or stellar job. Let anyone in. Played

through her mind again. When she reached the bathroom, she pulled out her phone and made another call.

"It hasn't even been ten minutes. I know I'm good but I'm not that good."

"Bryce –"

"BJ."

"Damn it, BJ! I need you to do me one more favor."

"Two favors in one day, what is this world coming to?"

"I need you to pull information on a person. I need this as soon as possible"

"Everything with you is as soon as possible. When do I ever receive a call from you that doesn't end with as soon as possible?

"BJ, this is life or death. I need you to focus and I need you to come through for me."

"I've got you covered. Who am I looking into?"

"Detective Robert Wilson."

THURSDAY, SEPTEMBER 19TH 9:45 P.M
DONATELLA'S CAR

Jasmyn and SA Dabria rode in a deafening silence for the first ten minutes after leaving the home of Sal Grandson. Jasmyn sensed the anguish radiating from the pores of her traveling companion. She stole a glance every few minutes but dared not speak. The intense squint and furrowed brows told her the gears were turning at an alarming speed, and she dare not cog the machine.

However, she was intrigued. Here sat a woman who less than two hours ago had been in what she would have considered a mortal battle. Yet she had the poise, grace, and fortitude to carry on as if nothing had ever happened.

"Yes?" she said, snapping Jasmyn out of her trance.

"Um, uh? Um what? Were you talking to me?" she stammered.

"You've subtly glanced over here five times in the last ten minutes, which tells me you have questions you'd like to have answered. So, what is it that you would like to know?"

"What is going on here? Children are disappearing, one already dead – bless his soul. Someone is reaching out to a journalist giving him the play-by-play. This all just seems like a bad dream that we are playing out in real life."

"Someone is using the children of Driftwood Springs as pawns in a sinister plot to hide their true intentions. They have been both devious and clever up to this point. They stay several moves ahead on this chess board, and they are moving ever so close to checkmate. Any additional mistakes will mean more children suffering."

"Sounds like you know why this is happening."

"Yes, I do."

"Do you know who is doing this?"

To this question Donatella did not immediately answer. Instead, her focus shifted beyond the windshield. "There are flashing lights coming from our subdivision."

"Oh my God. Do you think…" she involuntarily moved her hand over her stomach. "Do you think the email was right? Has another child been taken?" She could sense the bile dangling on her tonsils, and she swallowed air in an effort to push it down.

"Unfortunately, Mrs. Thompson, I believe more than the child's disappearance is at the root of those lights."

Jasmyn wearily looked over at Agent Dabria who simply continued to stare through the windshield as they drew closer towards the commotion in their community.

Thursday, September 19th – 9:45 p.m
Grant Residence (735 Franklin Lane)

"Douglas Grant, you are under arrest for the attempted abduction of Jeffery Carter."

"Doug!"

"Sylvia, call Poindexter."

"The kidnapping of Bree Singleton"

"Detective Wilson, what is the meaning of this? Why are you arresting my husband?"

"Sylvia, let the officer do his job."

"The kidnapping of Donny Taylor."

"Damn it, Sylvia, call Poindexter now!"

"And the murder of Thomas Grant."

"The murder of Thomas Grant!" Sylvia screamed at the top of her lungs. "What in the hell do you mean and the murder of Thomas Grant? Do you think Douglas had something to do with the murder of his own son? He was with me when Thomas disappeared!" She ran toward her husband in a desperate plea to have him released and to gain some understanding as to what she was being told.

"Mrs. Grant," Wilson said grabbing her gently by the elbow and pulling her away from her husband. "Do not make this any worse than it already is."

"Than it already is. THAN IT ALREADY IS! My son has been murdered and you are playing some demented joke by arresting my husband for his murder! I already told you, he was with me when Thomas disappeared."

"Sylvia, we think he had an accomplice. We will be going to make that arrest next."

"What accomplice?" She snarled a dribble of spit firing from her mouth landing on the lapel of Detective Wilson. "Accomplice. He couldn't have any accomplice, because he didn't do this."

The officer began to walk Douglas Grant out of the front door.

Yanking her arm free from Detective Wilson, Sylvia charged at the officer once again, "Release my husband now."

Wilson pulled her back, restraining her with both hands. "Look Sylvia, if I have to tell you again, you will be headed down to the station in cuffs along with Douglas. I suggest you do what Douglas has requested of you and make the call to your attorney. He will be going down to the station tonight and Poindexter can speak with him once he arrives. Until then, I'm going to respectfully ask you to stay out of our way."

Wilson released Sylvia Grants arms, walked out of the house, went down the stairs, and crossed over to his waiting squad car.

Thursday, September 19th – 10:00 p.m
Donatella's Car

As Jasmyn and Agent Dabria pulled into the community, Jasmyn realized that there were two distinct sets of light flashing. Neighbors had begun pouring out of their houses in an effort to ascertain the reason behind the commotion. Jasmyn turned the steering wheel three-quarters to the left when Agent Dabria said, "No, turn right."

"Shouldn't we turn left?" Interesting how this had turned into a "we" thing for her. She was excited and curious to see how this would all end before she settled back into her normal routine.

"I have no doubt if we turn left, we will see the police are preparing to arrest Douglas Grant, if they haven't already done so." She concluded. "However, a turn to the right may shed some additional light on the case."

Once again, Jasmyn glanced over at the agent and in a fluid motion rotated the steering wheel to the right and drove toward their next destination. Onlookers had made their way onto the sidewalk and into the streets. Jasmyn proceeded with caution, as the last thing she needed to do was clip a pedestrian with a federal agent in the car. Looking to her right she noticed, bathed in the yellowish glow from the sconces on either side of the garage, the woman with the fleshy ankles. The woman peered into the car in an attempt to discern both the driver and the passenger. She noticed Jasmyn first and immediately turned up her nose. Then upon noticing Donatella on the passenger side her eyes blazed, her puffy protruding lips parted mouthing "My God." She shifted her girth, turning her back to the car and stampeded up the driveway.

When Jasmyn drove by the house she shared with her husband, she saw Marcellous with his back turned to her while looking down the road towards the action. She tooted the horn twice, instantly gaining his attention and that of a few others as well. Maggie gave a whine followed by a bark as she saw her owner turn to look in her direction. Marcellous's eyes widened slightly when he realized it was his wife behind the wheel. He then gave a smirk when he saw the adjacent passenger, tilted his head forward with a nod and looked back down the road.

It didn't take long for Jasmyn to realize where this commotion originated, and it looked as if they were arriving at the epicenter. Being escorted from her house in black silk pajama bottoms and a long sleeve matching top was Diane Dresser. On the porch, Bill's arms gestured his confusion and frustration with the treatment his wife was enduring at the hands of the officer. From the beet red hue covering his cheeks and progressing towards the three creases adorning his forehead, it was evident his words were not moving the officers.

"There's nothing more here for us to see. Let's turn around. You can return to your home. I can manage to drive the remainder of the way back to my house."

"Not before you allow me to properly tend your wounds. I have everything I need in my medical kit at the house. I did a rush job when we were at your house, and if you are not going to the hospital then it's imperative that we properly clean, suture, and bandage your injuries."

Agent Dabria nodded her head in acquiescence, and the two made their way to the Thompson's residence where Jasmyn knew Marcellous would have a number of questions. And, to be honest, she was excited to tell him about the adventure she had been on for the last couple of hours.

12

THURSDAY, SEPTEMBER 19TH – 11:30 P.M
POLICE HQ (ONE POLICE PLAZA)

Douglas Grant sat isolated within Interrogation room #7 with a white foam cup of tepid black coffee perched directly in front of him. His wrists were cuffed together with a chain passing through a metal eye soldered to the table. He had just enough slack from the chain to bring the cup of coffee to his mouth if he bent his head forward a couple of inches. Grant warily peered toward the ceiling, thinking building services hadn't received the memo that fall had arrived.

The room, a 20x20 box was sparse with the HVAC vent placed just above the chair now occupied by Douglas Grant, was currently being pelted with a continuous stream of 63 degree forced air blowing into his face. After 240 seconds of this, he would receive a 30-second reprieve. Then the motor would reengage, and the air would begin its relentless assault once again.

Grant wasn't sure how long he had been left to sit in this frigid chamber. Twenty minutes, maybe thirty, he had lost track of time since they relieved him of his watch, belt, and shoes before dumping him in this room. Grant replayed the words of Detective Wilson, "...we think he had an accomplice. We will be going to make that arrest next."

The metal door of the room swung inward on well-worn, groaning hinges. Detective Wilson entered the room with his partner, Detective Ridder. Wilson sat in the chair directly across from Douglas, as Ridder dragged the chair from the corner generating a metallic screeching sound. Ridder sat his chair to the left of Wilson, placing himself between the door and their detainee.

"Douglas," Wilson started with a sympathetic tone. "This would go so much easier if you told us where Bree Singleton and Donny Taylor are being held." Grant had dealt with high stakes negotiations enough to know that it was better to keep his mouth shut and let the other party do all the talking. "There isn't anything we can do about the loss of Thomas, but no other children need to be harmed."

Grant had a mix of emotions run through his mind and over his face at the mention of Thomas. His wife had deceived him for years about the paternity of who he thought was his son. He was sure he would never forgive her for such a deception. Nonetheless, he loved Thomas as the only son he had ever known.

"Say something, you son of a bitch!" Ridder shouted. "We already have enough to fry you for what you've done to your own son."

Grant's eye twitched involuntarily.

"We simply want to know where the other two children are located!"

Grant mused internally, *this is a poor game of good cop,*

bad cop. He couldn't resist the urge to speak. "I have already asked for my lawyer, and I'm not saying a word to either of you until he arrives."

"You're only making this harder on yourself," Wilson stressed. "Since you are not in a talking mood, let me tell you what we know. Your wife states you were at home with her when Thomas, your son, disappeared. We believe this as fact. However, the whereabouts of your accomplice during his disappearance are shaky at best. We believe you had him abducted because you have known for some time that he was not your son. I still haven't put together how you found out he was not your son, but I'm confident you knew this prior to the conversation we had with your wife in your study. I'm also confident you didn't know who the father was, as I'm sure you would have dealt with this situation a lot differently."

Grant remained placid, staring directly into the eyes of Detective Wilson.

"You hatched a plan that would force your wife's hand to reveal publicly the truth of his paternity. You felt, and for this I'm guessing, that this would be the leverage you needed in order to divorce your wife and thus lesson the financial impact you would need to pay in a settlement. You figured you couldn't simply kidnap your child, as the spotlight would be intense, so you needed to kidnap another child. Mr. Grant, we have already checked with your office for the time of the disappearance of Bree Singleton. You were not in the office. If you were not in the office, where were you?"

Grant, recalling the sex he had with Diane that morning, made no effort to answer this question.

"I'm not sure how you were able to lure Bree into your car as she was an extremely cautious girl by nature. So, my guess is you blitzed her from behind somehow to gain the upper hand. Then I believe things began to unravel. Somehow, Thomas had become ill. From what our medical examiner has been able to determine, he came down with an aggressive case of pneumonia with bronchitis. The combination made it difficult for him to intake high levels of oxygen, and he keeled over while both you and your partner were away.

"With the realization of what happened, you both had a moment of panic and clarity. Disposing of the body at the Orbitz Technology Campus, a place for which you are certainly linked to, would steer light away from you – because why would you dispose of the body there? A place that any rational person would believe is the last place you would dump the body of your son. Crafty move to say the least, because it did just that. It had us thinking there was no way you could be involved with this kidnapping business."

Grant could feel his internal temperature rising.

"That brings us to the events of this evening, the attempted abduction of Jeffery Carter. Unlike the previous two abductions, Jeffery put up a heck of a fight. During this fight he managed to leave behind a piece of evidence. Our first true physical evidence in this case. You see, Douglas, I was the person who scared away his potential abductor. In a rush to leave the scene, Jeffery was able to pull from the wrist of the assailant this nice fine Rolex with an inscription on the back. Shall I read you the inscription, Mr. Grant?"

Grant's eyes, which were dull and inattentive during this monologue, were now glimmering as his eyelids narrowed. The last time he had seen this watch was three months ago. He and Diane had met at the Ritz-Carlton in Uptown Charlotte for an afternoon session prior to retiring back to their houses. He had always been careful not to leave anything behind. On this occasion as he was getting dressed, Diane began to nibble on his ear and then his neck. She insisted they still had more time, and she wanted a little more since it would be weeks before she could see him again. He protested, saying he wouldn't have time for another shower if they made love again. Sylvia would become suspicious if he arrived late without reason. She cooed, stating, "Who said you will need a shower?" as she slid off the bed, down between his legs, and unzipped his pants.

It wasn't until he was in his car around the corner from his house that he realized his watch was on the nightstand of the Ritz. He called the front desk and requested that his watch be held until he could pick it up the next day. To his astonishment, they said the watch was not there. He figured Diane must have seen it before she left the room. He gave her a call, and she too stated she had not seen the watch during her departure.

"To Douglas with love, Sylvia." Detective Wilson turned around the evidence bag and placed it close enough that Douglas would be able to read the inscription. He looked down, confirmed what he already knew was the truth on the back of the watch. At that moment he thought, *Diane, what have you done? You vindictive...*

"Is there anything you would like to say, Douglas?"

Wilson waited a few heartbeats. "No. Suit yourself. With the botched kidnapping of Jeffery Carter, it seems you had a moment of good fortune, as you ran across Donny Taylor, who was also on his way home. He never made it, and we want to know where you are holding him and Bree Singleton?"

He could hold in his fury no longer. "I have no clue what happened to Donny or Bree, and I certainly did not kill my own son!"

"He was not your son and I don't believe you killed him on purpose, but the truth of the matter is you killed him."

"I didn't kill anyone. You can state it until you are blue in the face. I haven't killed anyone and I didn't kidnap anyone."

"We have evidence linking you to the attempted kidnapping of Jeffery Carter and it won't be long before we find more evidence linking you to these disappearances."

"This evidence is manufactured!"

Storming through the door came Ashton Poindexter, who said, "This interview is over. Douglas, don't say another word."

Thursday, September 19th – 11:15 p.m
Donatella Residence (300 Calgary Lane)

DONATELLA PULLED her black Audi R8 coupe, fully loaded, black rims, smoked gray window tint and red calibers, into her three-car garage. When driven in the dark the car's profile reminded people of a bat flying sideways with its eyes blinking from the rotation of the tires against the calibers. She maneuvered the R8 into its normal location next to the Kawasaki ZX-6R motorcycle. Donatella shifted the transmission into park and stepped out of the car. With her left shoulder stinging from the pain of the knife wound, she reached across her body to activate the garage door button. The garage, which had been silent, was now filled with springs spinning, rotating the chains connected to the garage door. As the garage door continued to lower, Donatella opened the door to the house with her right hand, stepped into the house and shut the door behind her.

As she made her way to the kitchen, she recalled the events as they had taken place thus far, trying to make sense of the constant misdirection. *Why had another child been kidnapped if they already had Bree? Could it be to throw off the local PD?* Considering her suspicion of Detective Wilson, this seemed unlikely, but she began to wonder if she was mistaken.

Where were the kids, Bree and now Donny, being held? Bree, now missing for six days, could have been anywhere but was likely somewhere close by. Donny too would likely be nearby as it had only been a few hours since his disappearance.

How did this all tie back to Douglas Grant and Diane Dresser? Aside from their respective spouses sharing a kid together that seemingly neither one of them knew about, she didn't see a connection between the two. Could they have anything to do with the disappearance of the children that she had not yet put together? Was it possible that she was looking at this case all wrong?

She pulled open the door of her LG InstaView Door-in-Door Smart refrigerator, extracted an ice-cold Glaceu Smartwater, twisted off the cap, and took a drink. She walked toward the front of the house, mulling over the details again and again. Each turn she took led to more questions and fewer answers. Reaching the foyer, she instinctively moved her right hand up to her left shoulder and began to rub. She had to admit, Jasmyn had done a wonderful job stitching her up. She rather enjoyed the time she spent chatting with the Thompson family. She would need to go back and see them once this case was behind her.

Looking around, she noticed the crew removed the body and left no traces of blood anywhere on the floor. A new vase stood atop the table in the foyer adorned with fresh Blue Ocean Breeze Orchid. She smiled as she saw this and thought, *They remembered*. With that she continued to make her way up the stairs.

Once inside her room, she sat on the ottoman and removed her shoes. The phone rang. She glanced at the caller ID, stiffened her spine, forcing her to sit more erect, and answered.

"BJ, what do you have for me?"

"Well, good evening to you too, Agent Dabria. You know, it wouldn't hurt you to say hello every once in a while. It's simple. 'Hi BJ, how are you doing? How's your family doing? That's good to hear. Blah, Blah, Blah'. You are always so business-like."

"What do you have for me, Bryce?"

"B- Never mind. I looked into the details of the email Sal Grandson received from the anonymous sender. I have to say, whoever sent the email to Sal did one hell of a job hiding their steps. They had me hopping all over the world. It led me to a coffee shop located off of Trade St."

"And."

"I'm getting there. Geez! I was able to hack into their on-prem security system and download video for the last five days. I reviewed the video, keeping a close eye out for anything that might stick out during the time in which the email was sent. Indeed, I found a suspicious looking character. Suspicious in the sense they did everything to shield their face from the camera."

"Can you –"

"Yes, I've already sent the footage to you along with a couple of still photos. But I didn't stop there. I went back to the time in which you mentioned the first email was sent from Anonymous and repeated my review. Again, the same suspicious and shady character hiding from the camera. I sent that video to you as well."

"Anything on Detective Wilson?"

"Yeah. Let me see, where did I put it? Oh, there it is. Robert Wilson, who you know as Detective Wilson was born in Brooklyn, New York. His mother, a drug addict, died when he was two years old from an overdose. His father had been killed before Wilson was born. He was caught in the crossfire between two rival gangs on his way home from the grocery store.

With the death of his mother, Wilson was put into the system and lucky for him he was not there too long. He was adopted into a family that already had one boy and one girl. The family was well-to-do, and Robert obtained the best of everything. He eventually went to state college where he studied criminal justice. He left New York about ten years ago to take a position as a detective with the Charlotte Metro Police Department. He's been there since he left New York."

"What was the name of the family that adopted Wilson?"

"Let me see. It was, where is it at? Yeah, it was Mr. and Mrs. Anthony Carmichael."

"And their children?"

"The daughter, her name was Jane Carmichael. She married, a marriage that only lasted three years before ending in divorce, works as a journalist for the New York Times. She started her journalistic career under her married name, so she kept it instead of opting back to her maiden name. She goes by Markowitz. Jane Markowitz.

"The son, Clarence Carmichael, works as a big-time hedge fund manager on the New York Stock Exchange. Agent Dabria, let me tell you, this guy is loaded and doing well financially. Though I probably should not have looked, I couldn't resist. I looked at his finances. I haven't seen that many zeros since my time writing my algorithm to win the lottery. Anyway, I saw some weird transactions taking place, but I didn't look at it closely, as I had already been prying into the man's personal affairs."

As BJ was wrapping up his finding to Agent Dabria, she pulled out her laptop, willing it to move faster so that she could see the video. "Anything else, BJ?"

"No, Special Agent Dabria," he said in a robotic voice. "I have nothing more to share with you."

"You've done well," she responded in her familiar Southern drawl. "This information will prove to be of the utmost assistance. Thank you ever so much."

Before he could respond, she had disconnected the call and was pulling up the video. BJ had sent over two different video files, no doubt one from each day in which the suspect had been seen at the coffee shop. She queued the first video and pressed play.

BJ had clipped the first video down to one minute and twenty-seven seconds. She allowed the video to play from start to finish. The video showed a seated figured with their back to the camera wearing a black baseball cap and typing away on the computer. The figured reached a gloved hand out to pick up a cup of coffee, took a drink, and place the cup back onto the table. With this done, the figured continued to type for another twenty seconds before closing the laptop. Placing the device in a leather messenger bag, the figure stood up, slung the bag across their body with the strap on their left shoulder and the bag sitting just above their right hip and walked out the door, bag bouncing with each step. Donatella slid the slider on the video back to the point where the figure placed the laptop into the bag.

Again, the figured stood. Strap on left shoulder, bag on right hip bouncing as the figured walked out of the coffee shop. Donatella quickly queued the second video and pressed play. The figure, sitting in the exact same chair, except this time wearing a red baseball cap, was once again typing away on the keyboard. She noticed the duration on this video was slightly longer, one minute and forty-three seconds, but it was the exact same video. The figure reached out a gloved hand and took a drink of the coffee. At least this was what Donatella figured the patron was drinking since it was a coffee shop. The subject set the coffee back down on the table and typed some more. Then the figured placed the device in the same leather messenger bag, stood up, slung the bag across their body with the strap on their left shoulder and the bag sitting just above their right hip, and walked out the door, bag bouncing with each step.

Again, Donatella slid the slider on the video to the point where the figured placed the laptop in the bag and pressed play. Once the second video had concluded, Agent Dabria closed her laptop, followed by the closure of her eyes. She spoke out loud, "I know that walk – that limp."

13

FRIDAY, SEPTEMBER 20TH – 7:00 A.M
DONATELLA RESIDENCE (300 CALGARY LANE)

The next morning, Agent Dabria's head was spinning with the information she had received from BJ. The case itself was beginning to crystallize, except there were still some pieces that were not yet fitting together as seamlessly as she would have liked. Nonetheless, she was sure she would receive the answers she needed before the sun set on this day. One clue focused on the Carmichael child, and the other clue focused on the two videos she had received. The figure in the video could not be positively identified yet. Nonetheless, the limping gait of the figured was identification enough. She would need to make a stop first thing this morning to move the investigation forward.

She backed out of the garage and began to make her way down the street. While her first stop would be a brief drive, she would need her car for the next leg of her journey today. This stop brought her to the house of Detective Wilson. She shifted the car into park, opened the door, and stepped out of the vehicle. Standing at the mouth of the driveway, she didn't immediately proceed to the front door. Instead, she decided to walk around the grounds of the house and the entire property.

Agent Dabria started by walking around the right side of the house. As she did, she could hear the faint sounds of water running from the inside. Sounded like a shower, but she wasn't sure. Casually she strode as the sound of thunder began to serenade her ears. She took a look up to the sky and saw the pillow white puffs of clouds slowly turning gray. *Looks like we will get some rain tonight.* Dabria continued to walk as she came around to the back of the house. She looked out into the backyard. Nothing out of the ordinary. The patio consisted of a large barrel smoker, black wicker lounging furniture with red cushions, and an outdoor kitchen. Upon further inspection, it looked as if the patio had been extended to accommodate the kitchen as the cement seemed to have a cleaner sheen than what led from the house.

"Special Agent Dabria, is there something I can help you with this early in the morning?"

"Detective Wilson," she said, turning to face him. Wilson holding her gaze, held the back door open, sporting dark brown double-pleated dress slacks and a midnight-blue button-up long-sleeve dress shirt with only the top two buttons done. He was fiddling with the third button yet somehow continued to miss the hole by a fraction of an inch. His feet were bare, no shoes or socks, and he was sorely in need of a two-hour pedicure.

"I wanted to talk with you concerning the latest disappearance and the activity in the neighborhood last night. I'm curious about the suspects you apprehended. Do you mind if I come in, so we can continue to chat?"

Wilson gave her a distrusting glance as he pondered the question. "It would be nice if you called instead of just showing up."

"I originally planned to do just that until I realized I didn't have your cell phone number. Perhaps you can write it down and give it to me before I leave."

A flicker of disdain passed over his face that he attempted to mask, but Donatella spotted it as quickly as it had come, and just like that it had disappeared.

"Sure, come on in," he said, swinging the door wider and stepping aside so that she could enter.

Stepping past Wilson and into the house, she asked, "How long have you lived in here, in this house?"

"Coming up on six years," Wilson remarked as he followed Donatella toward the study. He could sense slight modulations in her head placement as if she were looking around.

"Are you the original owner? I know many of the people in the community built their houses."

"I am the original owner, though the house was built by another couple. They were unable to secure the financing, so I purchased the house from the bank. There were a few modifications I wanted to make, so I did them after I moved in. Like the extension of the patio. I wanted some additional space since I like to entertain outdoors."

Agent Dabria didn't say anything to this last comment. Instead, she turned into the study and took a seat. Detective Wilson walked around the large oak desk and settled into his desk chair.

"You made an arrest last night. Well, two arrests I should say. One was Mr. Douglas Grant, the father of the kidnapped and now deceased Thomas Grant."

Detective Wilson nodded his head.

"You also arrested Diane Dresser, whose husband, Bill Dresser is the biological father of Thomas Grant. What key piece of information am I missing that ties Mr. Grant and Mrs. Dresser to the death of Thomas Grant, the disappearance of Bree Singleton, and now the disappearance of Donny Taylor?"

"We haven't shared this news with the press, and we are keeping a tight lid on this at the station, so I will need to ask your discretion for what I'm about to tell you."

Agent Dabria placed her forefinger on top of her thumb, brought the fingers to her lips, moved them from left to right, twisted her wrist outward and flung her hand to the right as if she had just tossed something away. "Your secrets are secure with me, Detective Wilson."

"Douglas Grant and Diane Dresser have been having an affair. I haven't been able to pinpoint how long this has been taking place, but suffice it enough to say it's been going on for a lengthy amount of time."

Agent Dabria raised her eyebrow, placed her back against the back of the chair and shuffled her leg placement. She moved her right leg from atop her left leg and then crossed her left leg over her right.

"Our belief is the two of them wanted to be together, but with Douglas being the CEO of Orbitz Technology, he stood to lose a shit ton of money, excuse my French, in the divorce proceedings. It's likely he knew Thomas was not his son, but he didn't know the true paternity of the boy. He figured, and I'm guessing, that by kidnapping the boy Sylvia would need to confess and then he would release the boy. The fact that Thomas died we believe was an accident. The M.E. has concluded the boy died of pneumonia."

Agent Dabria shook her head as a sign to signify she was following the detective.

"We believe the kidnapping of Bree Hartley was to throw us a curveball. All along we have tried to find a connection between Thomas and Bree. There isn't one from what we can tell. Seems like it was done to have us waste time and energy. I presume the plan was to release both kids, Douglas would have grounds for divorce, and no one would be the wiser."

"And this new kidnapping victim. How exactly does he fit into your theory? Seems to me adding another victim was a risk Douglas and Diane didn't need to take, if your theory holds true."

"More misdirection," Wilson said. "Another kid meant another set of speculation and less talk about the death of Thomas. The latest victim, Donny, was not the originally intended victim."

Dabria raised her eyebrow again. Again, shifting the placement of her legs; however, in this case it was the reverse order. Left leg moved from atop the right leg. Right leg crossed over the left.

"Jeffery Carter was the intended victim. I was on my way home when I saw a guy struggling with a kid. My instincts kicked in, and I approached the vehicle. The assailant took off in his car. Unlike our other cases in which we didn't have any physical evidence, Jeffery managed to pull a Rolex watch off the wrist of the would-be kidnapper. I found the watch laying on the ground not far from where the attempted abduction was taking place. The watch was inscribed, 'To Douglas with love, Sylvia' and I knew we finally had our man."

"Great work, detective, but a couple of follow-up questions if I may. According to your theory, Douglas and Diane kidnapped Thomas and planned to give him back to his parents. How did they plan to do this without Thomas recognizing either one of them?"

"I didn't say they were the smartest criminals in the world. I'm not sure the best way to answer that question. I'm not sure there is even a good answer to be found."

"You stumbled across the attempted kidnapping of Jeffery Carter. Good thing you were there or he would have been missing. You let the kidnapper go, and he instead went on to kidnap Donny Taylor. Is there a reason you didn't go after the kidnapper instead of assisting Jeffery?"

"If I had it to do over, I certainly would have gone after the kidnapper. Had I done so, Donny would not be missing. At the time, I was more concerned with the safety of Jeffery, figuring the kidnapper would leave the community. I called dispatch to let them know what happened and figured the department could close in on him."

"I see. One final question. If Douglas Grant is your guy, he didn't have a lot of time to kidnap Donny and stash him prior to coming back home. Has your department concentrated the search in areas close to the subdivision?"

"We have, but we have not turned up any solid leads. I was pressing Douglas pretty hard until his attorney Ashton Poindexter walked in and put a stop to my interrogation. We had to call it a night, so I came home to refresh. I'll get another crack at him today. I'm sure I'll be able to break him."

Another sound of thunder cracked in the background as the daylight cascading in through the study window seemed to grow a little darker before going back to a full shine.

"Ahh. Well, that answers all of my questions. I thank you for your time." The two law enforcement officers stood and shook hands. "I can see myself out." And with that Agent Dabria made her way out of the study and out of the front door.

Detective Wilson picked up his cell phone and scrolled through his contact list. Finding the number he was searching for, he pressed the send button and placed the phone to his ear. The phone was answered on the third ring.

"She was just here going over the case and the recent arrest of Douglas and Diane."

After the person on the other end of the phone spoke, the detective went on.

"Yes, I think she bought it, but I think she is still suspicious. I caught her snooping around outside. When I brought her into the house, she had a curious eye."

His silence followed during the response.

"Agreed, she will need to be dealt with once and for all. I'll personally deal with her tonight."

FRIDAY, SEPTEMBER 20TH – 5:30 A.M
GRANDSON RESIDENCE (4208 JASPER ROAD)

Sal, a stickler to his routine woke up at 4:00 a.m for his five-mile jog. Today, however, the run was much slower than his normal pace. *Sal, you're losing it old buddy,* he thought, looking back at his run and analyzing his performance. *It's probably a result of how tired I was after the late night with the stunning Donatella and her friend Jillian. Wait, that wasn't her name. I think it was Jasmyn. I'm totally losing my edge. I cannot even keep names straight.*

Sal finished pulling on his khaki pants when his phone rang. He finished buttoning the pants and zipping the fly. He looked down at the screen of his cell phone, "Jane, calling again. She must be in town," he said aloud.

"Hello?"

"Sal, my dear! It's Jane. How the heck are you? I'm in town for a few days, and we absolutely need to get together. I'm not taking no for an answer."

"I'm not sure, Jane. I have a busy day ahead of me," he lied in an effort to steer her in a different direction.

Driftwood Springs

"Sal, how busy can you be that you cannot see an old friend? Why don't you meet me for coffee and a pastry?"

"Jane –"

"Sal, just say yes. You know how this game is played. You keep playing hard to get, I stay persistent, you eventually give, we have a good time, and there's a 60% chance we have a really good time."

"Alright, alright," Sal agreed reluctantly. The date was set and the phone disconnected.

Deep down in his core even if he couldn't allow the words to come out of his mouth or the thoughts to pass through his mind, but he really did want to see her. His computer chirped with an incoming email. Sal finished pulling on his socks before he made his way to the kitchen table to retrieve his email. He lowered himself into the wooden chair at the kitchen table, picked up his pen placing it into his mouth, and typed his password into his computer.

His email client was still open from the previous night when he shared the latest communication from Anonymous with Agent Dabria. He pulled the pen from his mouth, "Could this be another message from Anonymous?" He eyeballed the newest message "Protect your credit. Sign up for credit check now!" Sal hit the delete button.

"Nothing here to see." He angled his feet into his driving mocs, prepared to leave the house. He heard the rumble of thunder and looked out of the window, eyeballing the dark, ominous clouds. "Guess I better grab my umbrella." He looked down, reaching for his red golf umbrella. "On second thought." He shifted his hand to the right and pulled up his compact New York Daily umbrella and walked out of the door to meet Jane for coffee.

Friday, September 20th – 8:30 a.m
Brent's Coffee Shop (235 Trade St.)

Donatella was able to ID the coffee shop at 235 Trade Street that she received from BJ. She drove around the establishment twice in search of parking. She secured a spot two blocks away from her destination and proceeded East on Trade St. Heading to this coffee shop was a long shot, but Donatella needed answers. The mysterious woman from the video held the key to this mystery, and she was determined to locate her whereabouts. The sound of thunder crackled as Donatella crossed the street. She felt a single drop of rain splash across her right wrist as her arm swung in her now compromised walking motion. Although her left shoulder felt better as each hour passed by, she could still feel the twinge of pain if she jostled it too much.

A couple, a man in his early fifties and a girl in her late twenties came out of the coffee shop holding hands. As Donatella approached the door, he released the younger lady's hand and held the door open for the approaching beauty.

"After you, Ms.," he said, ushering her into the shop with his free hand. Donatella nodded her head in thanks and passed through the opening. As she did, the man fought the urge to turn and look in her direction. Instead, he released the door, interlacing his fingers between those of his companion, and they walked directly across the street to their vehicle.

The man helped the young lady into her seat, brushing his hand over her bottom as she bent down to sit. He made his way to the driver side, taking a whiff of his hand prior to dropping into his seat. He fired up the ignition, activated the turn signal, rotated the steering wheel, and pulled away from the curb. The now vacant spot was quickly filled by an oncoming black sedan. The driver of the sedan did not exit the vehicle, remaining seated instead with eyes fixated on the windows of the coffee shop.

Inside the coffee shop, Donatella stood third in line while waiting to be served by the pink haired, soft-spoken, lanky barista.

"Trevor is going to bring the entire department down." The man standing in front of her stated to his colleague. "I swear he is clueless in supply chain logistics, and if one more major client misses their shipment, there goes our business."

"Why doesn't Emily do something about it? I mean, she could fire him – right?"

"She should fire him! I don't think she will. Trevor's parents are tight with the owner, and I think Emily is afraid she will lose her job if she disciplines him strongly."

"Well maybe she should give him a different set of responsibilities. I don't want to lose my job over his ineptness. I'll take a double shot Espresso, with Skim milk, steamed with a sprinkle of cinnamon. I mean, come on, if he isn't getting the job done, he should be let go. Did you want something Charles?"

"Nope, I'm good. Just coming along for our daily why-doesn't-Emily-fire-Trevor conversation."

"That's all, hon, and I'm going to pay using my app."

As the woman dug into her purse looking for her phone, Donatella pulled out her FBI credentials and her phone. She located the picture she was searching for and held it at the ready for her turn at the counter.

"Next in line," the barista said, beaming at Donatella.

Donatella noticed the name tag pinned to the pink haired barista's shirt. "Margaret, my name is Special Agent Dabria," she said, flipping open her badge for the barista to inspect. "Do you mind if we take a step over to the side? I have a few questions I need to ask you concerning a patron who was here three days ago."

Margaret's eyes blazed with excitement. "Hmm sure," she said slightly above a whisper. "Let me find someone who can man the counter for me." She hurried away to an older man in the process of making the double espresso ordered by the woman in front of Donatella. Margaret said a couple of words and pointed in the direction of Donatella. After a brief exchange, Margaret removed her apron, walked from behind the counter and led Donatella over to a pair of chairs in the corner by the window facing the street.

"I'm so excited to be talking with you. This is the most exciting thing that's ever happened to me." The words came out in a hushed jumble. "Does this have anything to do with the disappearance of those children? The death of that poor little boy, Lord bless his soul. It must be serious if they have an FBI agent working the case."

On her drive over to the coffee shop, Agent Dabria had given BJ another call. She asked for him to send photos of anyone who was working the day the suspect came into the shop. One of the photos BJ sent over was that of Margaret.

Agent Dabria unlocked her cell phone, turned it around to the young girl. "Three days ago you served this woman." It was the picture of the suspect in the black baseball cap. "I need you to think back to the exchange with this woman and recall her face."

Donatella slid the display to the next picture. "Was this the woman you served?" Margaret looked earnestly at the photo, eyes squinting as she scanned the face.

"Honestly, I'm not sure. It kind of looks like her. If a positive identification is what you are looking for, you should ask Lave. He always notices the pretty women." Looking over her shoulder she spoke conspiratorially with a blush, "Lave, can you come over here for a minute? This lovely FBI agent has some questions she needs to have answered and you may be able to assist."

Lave, a handsomely rugged man in his late twenties with onyx black hair and dark set black eyes, looked up from his stocking duties and turned to the ladies sitting in the corner. When he stood to his full height, he was 6'2" with a swimmer's build. He excused himself as he brushed passed the woman with the double espresso and approached Agent Dabria and Margaret. Margaret slid left in the oversized chair, offering the other half to Lave, who acknowledged her with a head nod but opted to sit on the arm of the chair.

"Yes, ma'am, how can I help you?" he asked in deep voice that seemed to originate from within his core before escaping his vocal cords.

"My name is Special Agent Donatella Dabria," she stated as she flipped open her credentials. "I need you to look at this photo," she said, passing over her phone, "and tell me if you recognize this woman."

Lave looked over to Margaret, who eagerly shook her head in affirmation urging him to secure the phone. Lave looked back over to Donatella and reached his hand forward, clipping the table sitting next to him as he did. Shaking off the momentary sting, he grabbed the phone. He brought the phone closer to his face for a better look, tilting his head slightly to the left as if to gain a better view of the picture. Margaret, sensing some great revelation, sat on pins and needles, sliding to the edge of her chair with an ear to ear grin. Her eyes were fixed on every movement that Lave made and every breath that he took until he spoke.

"Yeah, I think I remember her. She's maybe a little older and her facial features have changed, but her eyes have not. We locked eyes once as she left from the counter with her coffee in hand. For that brief moment I was enchanted as her eyes continued to draw me in deeper. It was a feeling I had not felt before. Once our brief moment passed, she walked away, sitting in one of those chairs," he thumbed over his right shoulder with his right hand. "She then pulled out her computer and started to work."

Margaret's eyes twinkled as she exclaimed in her still whisper-like voice, "I knew Lave would recognize her!"

Special Agent Dabria eyed Lave for any sense of deception or uncertainty and saw none. Not realizing their conflict would come soon, Donatella handed both Margaret and Lave her card. "If she happens to come back, please give me a call. I ask that you do not approach her in any way."

Lave took the card from Agent Dabria's left hand and said, "Cool."

Margaret took the card from Agent Dabria's right hand, pulled it close to her bosom as if it was a precious family heirloom and said, "Yes ma'am, I mean Agent, I mean Special Agent. Yes, I will contact you should I see her again."

Donatella stood, thanking Margaret and Lave for their time. She floated through the crowd as she walked toward the exit with the feeling of dread. With her suspicions now confirmed, she needed to determine her next course of action. Looking out of the window, she could see a light drizzle of rain descending toward the ground. She pulled back the door so that she could exit and make her way west, back toward her car and ultimately her home.

Friday, September 20th – 8:30 a.m
Brent's Coffee Shop (235 Trade St.)

THE BLACK SEDAN sat outside of the coffee shop with the engine off and the occupant of the vehicle watching Agent Dabria through the stenciled glass windows. It was unlikely that the special agent was onto her, but it didn't really matter. Soon enough this drama would be coming to an end.

The occupant watched as Agent Dabria spoke to the pink-haired girl, *Margaret if I recall correctly*. The odds of Margaret remembering her was nil. Although little Ms. Margaret seemed like she was good at her job, she also seemed to be oblivious to the things that were going on around her. This was the reason the occupant came back to this particular coffee shop. The Wi-Fi, like in many other locations, was free and this particular barista wouldn't remember her face.

The two of them, Agent Dabria and Margaret sat in the corner chatting, and from the looks of it, Margaret was doing all the talking. Agent Dabria pulled the cellphone from her pocket and handed it to her seated companion. The lack of recognition could be read on her face from nearly thirty yards away. *No surprise*, the occupant thought. At that moment the younger girl called to someone else in the restaurant.

When the young man sat down, she immediately recognized him and felt he would probably recognize her. He was a handsome young man and their eyes had locked when she tried to pass him. *He's not likely to forget my face*, she thought as she gripped the steering wheel with both hands. The occupant watched the silent exchange between Donatella and the two employees of the coffee shop as her anxiety continued to rise.

Agent Dabria handed both Margaret and the young man her cards and begin to make her way to the door. The occupant saw lightning a few miles in the distance and a faint sign of rain gathering on her windshield. It looked as if she would need to accelerate her plans.

As Donatella headed west back to where her car was located, the occupant noticed Sal Grandson walking west as well. He was coming from the opposite direction, and therefore he and Donatella had not seen one another, and this gave her an idea for the next step in her plan.

15

FRIDAY, SEPTEMBER 20TH – 9:00 A.M
BRENT'S COFFEE SHOP (235 TRADE ST.)

Sal Grandson entered Brent's Coffee Shop, brushing away the residue of rain that accumulated in his brief jaunt from the car. Surveying his surroundings, he saw a pink-haired girl making her way behind the counter, retrieving an apron, and proceeding to the counter. The seat she occupied with a tall, gamely fellow had cleared once he went back to stocking coffee beans on the shelves. Sal took this as an opportunity to secure the seats they had vacated directly in front of the window.

He lowered himself into the oversized chair, setting his bag on the table and umbrella on the floor.

"On second thought, I'll sit my umbrella next to my bag on the table. No time like the present to remind Jane we are on opposite sides of this journalistic war."

"Still talking to yourself, I see," stated the throaty voice from over Sal's right shoulder.

Sal knew this voice. He loathed this voice. He loved this voice. He stood, turning to greet her, words stammering out as he did.

"Jane, I was just settling in." Jane Markowitz was the cool-shaded breeze on a humid summer day. She stood 5 foot 9, elegance in motion, with her pink Burberry spectacles perched against her high set cheekbones. Her hair, brunette, fell just below her earlobe providing an unobstructed view of her elongated neck. Around her neck she wore the pink and blue water drop pendant Sal had placed there one month before they broke things off. The tip of the pendant tantalized her cleavage formed by a flowing Lulus White Floral Print High-Low Maxi Dress. The straps crisscrossed at the back and draped over her slender shoulders.

Jane leaned, in cutting off his words, giving Sal a kiss on the left cheek, a kiss on the right cheek, and then embraced him with a hug. Sal could hear his heart rate, now at 124 beats per minute and rising, pulsating in his ears.

"Sal, my dear," she said, stepping back taking in the full picture of him. "You look wonderful, and you haven't changed a bit. Still rising before the roosters to get in your morning run?"

"Well, yeah," he said, heart rate now at 130. Inhaling to move some oxygen to his brain, "You look amazing yourself. Doesn't look like the Times is slowing you down one bit." Sal helped her to her seat before returning to his and moving the umbrella to the floor.

"Things at the Times are going well, but it's nothing like when you and I were battling it out for the front page of our respective papers. With the advent of social media, everyone is a journalist today. The role of your traditional press is changing bit by bit, or should I say byte by byte."

Sal caught the computer code reference and chuckled. It felt as if his heart rate had topped out and began going in the opposite direction. Jokingly, he said, "Hey now, don't forget I'm one of those non-traditional press social media types now."

"Sal," she said, brushing away his comment figuratively while brushing away a strand of hair literally. "You're different. You have journalistic integrity, and you find the source of truth before posting any articles you write. I'm sure you have noticed the trend, and knowing you like I do you have surveyed the landscape of your local social media counterparts and realized your writing far outpaces their writing. I check your site daily to see what you have written as part of my daily ritual. Shower, coffee, Sal's article for the day."

Heart rate elevating, this gruff journalist from New York City was beginning to blush with admiration.

"My brother, Clarence, has been intrigued with your work. Just recently, he reached out to me and asked for your phone number and email address. He said he wanted to pick your brain on an article you had written."

Strange, Sal thought. *I haven't heard from or talked to Clarence in years.* "When exactly did your brother request this information?"

"Hmm... Let me see. I'm pretty sure it was Sunday, September 15th. I was in the process of dressing for church. I remember because this was the first time I was heading to church in years. Two days prior on Friday the 13th, not one but two black cats crossed my path. Not only did they cross my path, they both stopped and looked at me with those yellow eyes. Now that I'm thinking about it, it could have been the same cat.

"Later that same day, I had my compact in my hand to freshen my makeup and it fell to the ground. I've dropped this damn thing several times before, yet on this day it decided to break – into thirteen pieces.

"The last straw came later that evening. I was out to dinner with a few girlfriends, having a drink to celebrate the end of a stressful work week. I was leading our group to the exit, so we could all make our way home. A man was working on the signage that sits above the door when all of a sudden he lost his balance and the ladder came crashing down in front of me. Three seconds later and that ladder would have fallen directly onto my head.

"At that moment I decided I need to seek the Lord. Sal Grandson, you know I'm not the superstitious type, but that was way too many coincidences for me to ignore. So, on that Sunday I made my way to church, and as I said I received a call from Clarence that same day looking for your information."

"I don't believe in coincidences either," Sal mumbled under his breath.

"What was that hon?"

"I said that could have taken you to your death. I'm glad you are alright. Did your brother happen to say which article he wanted to ask me about?"

"You haven't talked to him? With him calling me as early in the morning as he did, I figured it was a pressing issue and that he planned to contact you that day."

"No, I haven't spoken with him. Maybe I just missed his call," he covered. But his mind was working overtime. Why would Jane's brother, a person he has no relationship with, all of a sudden want to reach out to ask him about a vague article? A request he made a day after the article detailing the disappearance of Thomas Grant. A request he made just days prior to the first Anonymous correspondence he received.

"Anyway Sal, I know you are wondering why I asked to meet with you. I miss you, Sal bear. I know it's mainly my fault how things ended the way they did, and I should not have thrown that plate at your head. And the saucer and the coffee cup. What I'm saying is you were the best thing that ever happened to me on a personal level. You challenged me mentally, you understood me professionally, and you made love to me with a fire and ferocity that left my leg tingling for hours. I know I'm putting you on the spot, and I don't need you to answer me at this minute. I know you will need to think about it, nonetheless I wanted to put my feelings out into the universe in the hopes that one day you will be able to love me again."

Sal had a feeling the conversation would journey down this path, yet hearing the words from her mouth left him speechless. This was a feat that no one other than Jane ever had on him, and though it didn't happen often, when it did he was truly paralyzed.

"Jane, I'm not sure what to say. Give me some time to think about it." What Sal really wanted to do was tell her how he too had missed her, but not now. Not at this moment. He had to focus on this new bit of information that was passed his way, and he could not stay distracted.

"I understand," she said as she began to stand. "I'll give you some time, but don't leave me in the wind too long." Jane bent at the waist, her face mere inches from Sal's. He felt she was going to double kiss his cheeks, but she looked him in the eyes, enchanting him in her stare, and kissed him fully on the lips. With his heart rate pounding feverishly, he kissed her back. He could feel the electricity from her lips as the thunder cascaded in the background.

As Jane pulled away, her bottom lip tacked to his for a brief moment, he opened his eyes that he didn't recall closing. She stood and made her way to the exit. Sal was too blown away to make a move and sat in his trance-like state for several minutes after her departure. The phone vibrating on his hip brought him back to reality. He reached into his pocket to see that he had a text message.

"If you want to know why those children have been targeted, meet me at the public library on 3rd and Cornell. No cops."

Sal's heart, which was racing from the kiss he received from Jane, was now racing for another reason. He had a chance to finally meet this mysterious anonymous person, and for now he would play by their rules. He would call Agent Dabria after the meeting, after he could obtain clarity about this case in time to write his next article.

Thunder crackled in the background, as lightning filled the sky. The midst of rain Sal encountered upon his arrival at the coffee shop had now turned into a constant downpour. Sal retrieved his bag from the table and his New York Daily umbrella from the floor and proceeded toward the exit. Once at the door, he opened up the umbrella, stepped out into the rain, and made his way east toward his vehicle.

Several thoughts were now swirling through his head. He could finally break open this case if this Anonymous person could supply the goods, something he believed to be plausible considering they had been right each time thus far. He was also thinking about his conversation with Jane, the kiss he received from Jane. He was thinking about the scent he hadn't noticed at the time, but he could now sense around him. He was...

Sal felt a sharp sting to the left side of his neck as he walked. He felt fluid being pressed under his skin where the pain had originated. He turned his head in an effort to see what had caused this pain. Before his world went black, he saw her. "It's you!"

16

FRIDAY, SEPTEMBER 20TH – 8:00 P.M
DONATELLA RESIDENCE (300 CALGARY LANE)

Donatella stood in her closet, her personal gear laid out in front of her. She stared at the picture in her hand of her holding Bree as a baby. It was time she pressed the issue regardless of how many feathers it ruffled. She thought back to the conversation she had with Bree prior to their relocation into the Witness Protection Program.

"God mommy, is it safe where we are going to?"

"It's safe, sweetheart, and you'll get the chance to meet all kinds of new friends and live in a really secure neighborhood."

"I overheard mommy and daddy saying we had to move, and we would need to get used to using our new names. Mommy was worried about the stress daddy was under, and he said everything would be okay."

"Now Bree, did you overhear the conversation by accident or were you sneaking somewhere you were not supposed to be listening to their conversation?"

"Well, I guess I was listening when I was not supposed to be."

"That's what I figured. Anyway, your daddy is a smart guy, a good guy. He is doing something courageous to help God mommy take down some bad people."

"Really? That is so cool. Will he get to wear a gun just like you?"

"No, Bree, my dear. He will not get to wear a gun. But you should be very proud of him. I know this is a lot to pick up and move, but I will be there every step of the way, keeping you safe."

"Pinky promise?"

"Pinky promise!"

"Will you bring your guns as well?"

"Girl, what is it with you and the fascination you have with guns? But to answer your question, yes, I will have my guns along with other items with me. Now, it's time for you to go to sleep. Moving day is tomorrow, and I want you fresh for the trip."

"Yes, ma'am."

DONATELLA PLACED the picture back into her shoe box, placed it on the top shelf and looked over her gear one more time. Donatella heard the chime from a door opening followed by the audible mechanical voice, "Morning room door opened."

The thought ran quickly through Donatella's mind, *who in the hell just walked into my house?* She didn't let the thought linger longer than it took to conjure in her mind. She immediately moved into fight mode. She placed her utility belt around her narrow waist, securing it with the latch as it sunk slightly down to her hips. Her utility belt had a holster for her FBI issued Sig Sauer P226 9 mm semiautomatic handgun, slots for two extra clips, her set of twelve Japanese Shinobi throwing knives, and an ASP 21" Expandable Baton.

Donatella pulled one of the Shinobi throwing knives from its leather sheath with her right hand as she opened her bedroom door with her left hand. She approached the double helix stairway when a pistol shot whizzed by her ear, impacting the drywall behind her.

Two more shots rang out as Donatella dropped to the ground, shots flying harmlessly over her head. She army-crawled beyond the opening of the stairs as she heard footsteps running up the left side. She wasn't sure if this was the work of one intruder or multiple intruders, but she had to determine the playing field she was dealing with at the moment. Once she cleared the opening to the stairs, she sprung to her feet and took off in a full sprint.

She heard two more shots explode from the barrel of the gun.

BANG! BANG!

Both shot missed to her right, sending shards of drywall cascading toward her feet as the intruder running up the stairs didn't have time to sight her properly. Donatella made it to the back of the house and the second set of stairs. This was her house, and she knew it better than anyone else. She descended the steps, placing the throwing knife back into its sheath and extracted her Sig Sauer. She racked it once to ensure a round was in the chamber as she reached the bottom step. She didn't hear any footfalls overhead, which meant the assailant either stopped on the stairway or made their way down to the first floor as well.

She allowed her gun to lead the way into the kitchen, eyes scanning back and forth quickly for any immediate threats. She saw none, but she did recognize a foreign smell out of place in her dwellings. She flattened herself against the wall and watched the reflection in the microwave for any signs of life moving beyond her vision. She could see a shadowy figure in a mask stepping slowly from her formal dining room into the study. She pushed herself from the wall, spinning 180 degrees while dropping to one knee and fired off two shots from her Sig Sauer semiautomatic handgun.

BANG! BANG!

The shots broke the silence and in reaction to the sound the assailant let off one round that flew harmlessly into the kitchen and past Donatella. The shots Donatella fired both ended in distinct sounds. The first was the sound of her glass vase shattering. She shook her head, realizing her Blue Ocean Breeze Orchids would need to be replaced again.

The second sound was that of the bullet hitting cloth and skin. Though she turned the corner and fired somewhat blindly, she figured the second shot hit the intruder in the leg. As she looked down the hall, she could see a small trail of blood entering into the study. The study had two exits, one back into the foyer and the other leading toward the family room.

Donatella, now the hunter and not the prey, advanced down the foyer. Although she was confident there was only one person in the house, she didn't take anything for granted. She peered into the formal dining room to ensure there wasn't another intruder waiting to ambush her the minute she turned her back to enter the study. She was rewarded with the sight of an empty room, so she turned her attention back to the study.

She looked down and noticed a much larger pool of blood than she had expected. Donatella entered the room and, on the ground, lay her assailant, applying pressure to his leg. Blood gushed uncontrollably through his fingers. Donatella rushed over to the intruder, Sig Sauer in her right hand leveled at his head as she removed the mask.

"Where is she? Where is Bree and where is Donny? Damn it, Wilson, speak."

Detective Rob Wilson, eyes large and staring at Donatella, tried to form words. Donatella could tell he was losing blood fast. From the looks of it, she hit Wilson in the femoral artery of his left leg. She pulled her shirt from over her head and tied the cloth quickly around his leg.

"Wilson, you're going to bleed out," Donatella said in a detached voice. "From the amount of blood you've already lost, you have a minute maybe two at best before you lose consciousness. Do something right. Where are the kids?"

"I never meant for any of this to happen," Wilson said, blood still pulsating through his fingers but not at the rate it was previously. "This was his idea."

"Yes, I know. I was able to put it together. Clarence Carmichael, your stepbrother has set these terrible plans in motion. At this moment, that's not important. Where are the kids?"

Wilson looked at Donatella, pondering if he should tell her or if he should take this secret to his grave. His eyes obtained the steely focus; he had made up his mind.

"You'll need to," he coughed up blood, eyes trying to roll to the back of his head as he fought to keep them in place.

"House. House." He slumped over. Donatella shook him, but he was gone.

Donatella sprinted down the hallway to the garage, ignoring the pain shooting from her left shoulder. She depressed the garage door opener attached to the wall, jumped into her Audi R8, and fired up the engine. When the garage door was open enough to allow the sleek coupe to fit underneath, she slammed her foot on the accelerator and shot out of the garage. She raced down the street, making her way to Wilson's house.

Once she arrived at his house, she slammed the selector into park and rushed out of the car. In an all-out sprint from the driveway to his front door, Agent Dabria pulled the Sig Sauer from her hip, fired three rounds into the locking mechanism and used her momentum to carry her through the wooden door.

The house was dark and silent.

"Bree, are you here? Can you hear me?" She ran full speed up the stairs, taking two at a time while fearing the worst but hoping for the best. When she hit the top of the stairs, she shot forward to the room on the right. Adrenaline coursing through her veins, she kicked the door open and flipped the light switch.

"Shit!" Empty.

She turned to the room across the hall. This door too was closed. This time she reached out for the handle and turned the knob. The door was unlocked. She flung the door open and flipped on the light. Empty.

She looked down the hall and saw there were two more

rooms. She raced to the room on the left side of the hall, turned the knob, and pushed the door open. This room too was dark, so she switched on the light. Empty.

"Damn it! Bree. Can you hear me? Bree!" She faced the last door on this floor, the master bedroom. She turned the knob. Locked! *What the hell? You sick bastard, if you touched her.* She didn't even finish the thought. At this moment Wilson was likely officially lying dead in her study. Not wanting to endanger Bree if she was in the room, she holstered her weapon and kicked at the double door. The door groaned on its hinges but did not give way. She took three steps back, gained some momentum, and kicked into the center of the double doors. Both doors shot open, flying inward at opposite directions and providing clear vision into the room. The light to this room was already illuminated. Frantically she surveyed the room in mild disbelief and yet relieved, *Bree is not in here.*

She stood isolated in the center of the room, taking shallow breaths, adrenaline pumping. She racked her brain. *Wilson uttered the word house twice before he expired. He surly meant his house.* At that moment she remembered the incongruent patio she noticed toward the back of the house. Donatella spun on her heels and sprinted down the hall and back down the steps.

"Bree! Can you hear me? Bree!" she yelled as she approached the kitchen. She turned on all the lights so that she could get a better view of the room. The left side of the room had a wall extended into the kitchen that destroyed the symmetry. Though stylishly decorated, now that she was looking for it, it was out of place.

Agent Dabria walked over to the wall, first looking at it for any tell-tell sign of a passage. Seeing nothing obvious she began to feel around. After a minute of feeling all over the wall she had nothing. She leaned back against the island and stared at the wall, willing something, anything to happen. In the corner between the wall and the window she noticed an electrical outlet. This was an AFCI Outlet that consisted of the Reset and Test buttons. These outlets were used to prevent electrical surges by automatically tripping if too much power was flowing through the circuit. If the outlet tripped, the Reset button extended outward and displayed a red light.

As Donatella eyeballed this outlet, she realized the Reset button was standing out, yet the light was not on. She walked over to the outlet and depressed the button. Donatella heard the click behind the button and was also rewarded with a latch unlocking on the side of the wall. Donatella hastily moved around the corner and saw that the smooth wall had given way to a door that cracked open by six inches.

Agent Dabria pulled the door open enough to move her frame through the door, felt around for a switch, and turned on the light. What lay before her was a set of stairs leading underground. Dabria rushed down the stairs, eyes scanning for any threats, though she figured she would not run into any down here. The temperature dropped twenty degrees by the time she reached the bottom.

Before her, twenty yards away stood a single door bolted shut with a stainless-steel security latch.

"Bree!" Donatella yelled, running toward the door. "Bree, I'm here!" She unlatched the door and pushed it open. In the corner, lay a figure unmoving. "Bree!" Donatella exhaled covering the few feet over to the figure and dropping to her knees. "Bree, I'm here," she said turning the figure over to face her.

Horrified, she looked at the figured, who was breathing and still alive. "Donny!" She stood, turning circles in the room. The room contained no additional occupants. Donatella dropped back to her knees. "Donny, have you seen Bree? Has anyone else been here?"

Donny's eyes flicked open and he croaked out, "No." Donatella dropped her head into her hands. *Where else could she be?*

Her cellphone rang. She pulled the phone from her pocket, looked at the number, "Private." She pressed send on the phone and pulled the phone to her ear.

"Special Agent Donatella Dabria," the crisp, cool voice chided from the other side. Since you are there with Donny, I assume you have dispatched with Detective Wilson. I knew he would blunder this too. But you need not worry. I have your precious Bree here with me!"

Donatella leapt to her feet. "Where are you?"

"Don't worry, I have every intention of telling you exactly where I am, and if you play by my rules you can save your precious Goddaughter."

Donatella squeezed the cellphone until her knuckles began to hurt.

"Come to the new Orbitz Technology Campus, Building 1, alone. The clock is already ticking."

The line went dead. Donatella looked down to the boy. "Can you walk?"

"Yes," he said with a little more strength in his voice than the first time he spoke.

"Good! I need you to make your way up the stairs and call your parents to come and get you. Once they come then they can call the police. Am I clear?" she asked in a rush.

"Yes."

"I'm going to leave you. Get moving." She turned swiftly and began running out of the door.

"Thank you." The sound of his weak voice trailed behind her as she raced back up the stairs.

17
FRIDAY, SEPTEMBER 20TH – 10:30 P.M
ORBITZ TECHNOLOGY CAMPUS

The dark gray clouds that sprawled ominously in the starless night over the city released rain that relentlessly pounded the pavement. Donatella parked her Audi thirty meters from the entrance of the Orbitz Technology Campus and stepped into the pouring rain. Unsure what she would be faced with once she crossed the threshold of the building, she hurriedly took reconnaissance of the grounds. She bypassed the construction-grade trash receptacle that consumed the lifeless body of Thomas Grant.

Keep your mind clear, she reminded herself. *I will not let the same happen to Bree.*

She pulled the soaking wet hair that framed her face from her eyes and quickly placed each strand into a ponytail. Rain pelting her exposed forehead, she continued to traverse the grounds carefully observing her terrain and environment. She noticed precut lumber exposed from underneath a navy-blue tarp piled against the building. Next to this pile were discarded boxes that previously contained smart boards that would grace each room within the center.

Donatella turned the final corner appearing back at the entrance into Building 1. She closed her eyes, inhaled a long, deep breath, and slowly released the air from her lungs and the tension from her body. She pulled back on the metal door handle with "OTC" etched into the surface and walked into the building.

The lobby sat bathed in the glow from the three oversized projector screens that each encompassed one white word on a royal blue background. The projector screen on the left had the word "Orbitz." The projector screen in the middle had the word "Technology." The projector screen on the right had the word "Campus." The glow provided the dim outline of a catwalk connecting the right half of the building with the left half of the building. Donatella's bat-like eyes quickly adjusted to the impaling darkness and more of the surroundings came into focus. Badge-reading electronic turnstiles anchored the major pathway on the right and the left side of the atrium. The remainder of the atrium appeared lifeless given its enormous size until a voice came bellowing from the unseen sound system.

"Special Agent Donatella Dabria of the famed FBI, it took you long enough to join us."

The voice, a voice that Donatella recognized from the past grated in her ears. "Former Special Agent Terri Buckley," she said in her Southern drawl.

"Ah, no doubt you would figure it out, but I must say it took you much longer than I would have expected from someone of your caliber. I guess you're getting sloppy, or is it you simply are not as good as everyone made you out to be?"

"We don't have time for this. Where is Bree?" demanded Agent Dabria.

"We don't have time for this?" boomed the disembodied voice. "You are not in control of this situation! I am in control, and we have as much time as I deem necessary! Now, where was I?" she asked, back in her matter of fact voice. "That's right, you and your diminishing skills. The skills you felt was so much better than mine that you had me removed as your partner. Do you have any idea the stain that put on my reputation?"

SA Dabria spied the atrium, looking for any clues as to where Bree was being held. As she peered, she spoke, "Buckley, you were beginning to lose control. In fact, you had lost control. Your actions in the Alexander case was the first warning I should have paid closer attention to at the time. As your partner, we discussed your actions and you assured me it was a one-time thing, a blip on the radar. You would see the psychiatrist and work through the anger that was resonating within you. I trusted you. I trusted your word.

"Then came the Smithville case. What you did is both unforgivable and in my mind grounds for termination. However, the bureau felt disciplinary actions were enough and you were allowed to keep your job. But that job would not see me as your partner."

"Goody two shoe Dabria," Buckley spit into the microphone. "You always think you know best. Should I remind you of the actions you took against our weapons-smuggling friend Pablo Rodriquez? If I recall correctly, what you did in that case was not by the books. It's laughable how you think the rules only apply to everyone else. However, if it's something that Donatella wants, it's what Donatella gets. Well, damn it, not today. Today, I get what I want."

The left projector screen flicked, and an image replaced the word "Orbitz" on the screen. Donatella had no trouble recognizing the form that appeared tied to a chair on the screen. Bree Huntley sat with mouth gagged, hands tied behind her back, and ankles restrained to a metal chair that was bolted to the middle of a room. Donatella stiffened.

"You're precious Goddaughter is alive and well, at least for the time being. We will get to that in a moment. Seems like her father Frank got involved with some, shall we say, shifty characters. Clarence Carmichael, while on the surface is a brilliant hedge fund manager, had a shady business on the side. Insider trading is one thing, and let's be honest with one another, he's not the only one on Wall Street manipulating the system. But that isn't what had old Mr. Huntley up in arms. No, he found out a more devious plan that had been hatched by Mr. Carmichael."

Donatella transfixed on the image of Bree plastered on the screen, the fury coursing through her veins manifested with the vein on her temple pulsating. She clinched her fist as she listened to the dissertation from Buckley.

"Dear Mr. Clarence Carmichael decided he wanted excitement in his life that wasn't being fulfilled with his day trading job. So, he decided to move white powder. He started small in his native New York, then decided to go regional. His success at its apex, he decided to cover North America, including Canada. This last strategic move is what ultimately landed him in the mess he is in now. Stupid man got in over his head transacting business while at work. Lord he obviously wanted to be caught behaving so recklessly.

"Huntley reached out to his wife's dear friend with the FBI, and she launched a one-man, or should I say a one-woman, investigation. The rest as they say is history. You were able to dig and find some proof, but you needed Huntley to testify in order to seal the deal. You once again had your subject in your crosshairs. Your spotless, perfect record on the line, as you would be helping out a family friend. You pressed the bureau and they agreed for the safety of Liz, Frank, and your precious Goddaughter, they would place them into witness protection until the trial. Carmichael, at the end of his rope, reached out to my employer. Oh! That's right, you haven't been brought up to speed on who pays for my services these days. Well, that, my friend, is a doozy.

"An outfit that you are intimately familiar with heard I had been let go by the bureau and decided they could use someone with my skill set. You know, the same skill set you deemed unworthy to work alongside you. They didn't see it this way. They saw the can-do, stop-at-nothing work ethic I employed to get the job done, regardless of who or what stood in my way. And frankly at this moment you are the one standing in my way. But I digress.

"They also let me in on a little secret. One that I knew about in only sparse details, but now I know the full story. You know the story. Man and woman depart for a business trip leaving their only daughter behind."

Donatella's eyes widened and her heart rate began to spike.

"Man and woman board a luxury boat, boat goes boom, daughter left as an orphan to be raised by her aunt. This after school special is brought to you by The Syndicate."

"You wretched, despicable bi –"

"Tisk, tisk SA Dabria. Is that the way to talk to a suspect? Maybe you are unfit to serve in the bureau. Maybe I should take that up with your superiors," Buckley countered in a sarcastic tone. "They told me all about how they planned it, and how still to this day no one has a clue how they did it. Well I do and I must say, it was masterful. A work of extraordinary brilliance. But that is not why we are here today. Maybe one day we can sit down over crumpets and tea and I can fill you in on the gory details. Today SA Dabria, we are here for me to see you fail."

The projector screen on the right side of the atrium flickered, and the word "Campus" was replaced with a new image. This image was of another figure secured to a metal chair in the same manner as Bree. Momentarily, Donatella didn't recognize the figure until his head was lifted. Sal Grandson sat gagged in his chair, looking around and trying to ascertain his location.

"I'm sure you are familiar with our friendly journalist Salvatore "Sal" Grandson. I must say he has been extremely useful in this endeavor. Who would have guessed that Clarence's sister, who had a close relationship with Sal, would come in so handy? A simple request from her eldest brother to reach out to the journalist and voila, we had a way to control the narrative. Some call it dumb luck, but me, I'm going to side with divine intervention, because God himself doesn't want to see you succeed. He is a vengeful God, and no one is perfect other than he. Nonetheless, Sal unwittingly has been doing work for The Syndicate, but it seemed as if he was about to figure us out.

"Seems like Clarence's call to his sister rekindled the lost feelings she had for Sal. The thought of it makes me want to puke, but to each her own. She decided to traipse down here to North Carolina, meet Sal, and I'm pretty darn sure she would have brought up the fact her brother wanted to reach out to him for a story. For better or worse, Sal isn't an utter fool and I'm sure he would have put two and two together. Then he likely would have reached out to you, and my plan would have been ruined. So, I kidnapped him, right off of the streets and no one even saw it. Damn I'm good."

"What about Detective Wilson?" Donatella asked, interrupting the speaker. "How did he play into your sick, demented plan?"

"Oh yes, poor Detective Wilson, the man you killed earlier today, if I'm not mistaken. He had the simple job of kidnapping the kids and ensuring they were returned to their families once the trial had ended. This was to keep the local law enforcement focused on a potential serial kidnapper while we were able to use the disappearance of Bree to keep the Huntley's from showing back up in New York to testify.

"Wilson pretty much had the lay of the neighborhood and knew just about every secret within Driftwood Springs. Carmichael had been subsidizing the living quarters for Wilson for years. Though he was adopted, he was treated like family and both Jane and Clarence truly cared for their adopted brother. Since Clarence had been subsidizing Wilson's living for so long, he called in a favor and reminded his baby brother how much he had shelled out over the years to take care of his needs. After a week of pressure, he finally caved with the agreement no one would be hurt.

"The Grant's were by far the most intriguing. A son conceived from a one-night stand Sylvia Grant had many years ago. Her husband, Douglas Grant having an affair with the woman, Diane Dresser, whose husband Bill was the biological father of Thomas Grant. You can't make this shit up!

"Then you have Jeffery Carter. His dad regularly beats him and his mom after a night out drinking with his high school buddies. He blamed his wife for not being further in life than he was at this moment. A loser who wanted to blame his wife and kids for his failures. I may go end his existence after we are done here.

"Then there is Donny Taylor. While it seemed to the outside world it was a kidnapping of opportunity, he was indeed the target and not Jeffery Carter. Jeffery was a ploy to plant evidence against Thomas Grant. We needed a way for the kidnapping failure of Jeffery to play into the narrative. Donny's mother knows his secret, yet she refused to address it. Donny was being molested by his uncle, his mother's brother. That sick fuck needs to be castrated, and maybe I'll add him to my list as well. The kidnapping of Donny is probably a mercy for that poor boy.

"But Wilson, the forever fuck up, allowed Thomas Grant to come down with pneumonia in September. How in the hell does someone catch pneumonia in the middle of September? Nonetheless, Thomas died, and we had to help Rob clean up the mess, which leads us back to your Mr. Sal Grandson and why he's here. But enough of this, shall we get down to business?"

"By all means," stated Dabria

FRIDAY, SEPTEMBER 20TH – 11:00 P.M
ORBITZ TECHNOLOGY CAMPUS

"Let's play a game, you and I," stated Buckley. "The stakes of this game, life or death. As you can easily discern from the atrium, this building is split up into two distinct sides. On your left-hand side, you will find your beloved Goddaughter, Bree. You can see from the video feed, she is alive and well. What you don't see is the C4 that is plastered to the bottom of her chair. It's enough to kill her and take out the entire left side of the building.

"On your right-hand side, you'll find Sal Grandson. Undoubtedly you can see he too is alive, and similarly to Ms. Bree he also has C4 strapped to the bottom of his chair. Again, enough to kill him and take out his side of the building, but the other side will be spared.

"Now bring your attention to the center screen. The screen that displayed the word 'Technology' was now replaced with a timer that read 30:00. I see your little mind already at work. Thirty minutes is enough time to go up one side to save Bree and then go up the other side to save Sal.

But that wouldn't be a fun game. Waiting patiently on each side of the building is a set of well-trained assassins loyal to The Syndicate. Their job is to prevent you from reaching the floor holding the captives. I have sparred with a couple of them, and let me tell you they can pack a punch."

Donatella heard a faint buzz and then the atrium was illuminated in lights.

"Allow me to draw your attention to the left side of the atrium and the right side of the atrium. You'll notice that each side has an electronic turnstile gate, but this isn't your average turnstile. We've taken some time to retrofit the electronics within the turnstiles with metal detectors. Those metal detectors are linked to the countdown timer. If it detects any metal on your person, your gun for example, it will chime and five minutes will be deducted from your remaining time.

"Being the sport that I am, I'll give you a shot at a bonus. If you make it to the top to save one of your hostages, I will remotely disarm the bomb. In doing so, you will be granted ten additional minutes. At which point, you have a decision to make. Do you attempt to save the other person, or do you sentence them to their death? But make no mistake, you will need to fight your way to the top in order to save the second person as well. The second team will be motivated considering you would have dispatched with their compadres.

"Agent Dabria, you cannot save them both. The math doesn't work for you. Either you die trying to save the first hostage, which in that case all three of you will die. You save the first hostage and you make it to safety knowing the second hostage will die. Or you try to play superhero and make your way for the second hostage and you both die, as time will surely run out. And frankly Donatella, I don't care! I don't care which decision you make. I don't care what happens to Bree and I don't care what happens to Sal. I do care that your spot-free record will be spotless no more."

The sound from the PA ceased and the clock ticked down 29:59, 29:58. Donatella unfastened her utility belt and let it drop to the floor. She sprinted to the left side, passing through the electronic turnstile that greeted her with silence. She ran to the elevator and hit the up arrow. Nothing. She saw the universal sign for stairs at the end of the elevator corridor and took off again in a sprint.

Donatella's mind raced as each foot pounded the marble flooring. *What does Buckley have planned? Can she be trusted? How many people do I need to face-off with until I reach Bree? Will I have enough time to reach Bree and possibly Sal as well?*

She burst through the door to the stairwell and took two steps at a time. 2, 4, 6, 8, 10, 12. She hit the landing, made the ninety-degree turn to hit the next set. 2, 4, 6, 8, 10, 12, 14. The stairway leading from the second floor to the third floor had been barricaded by some makeshift contraption and locking mechanism. Donatella turned, facing the door stilling herself for the conflict lurking beyond. She turned the handle downward, pulled the door open, and stepped onto the floor.

Special Agent Dabria's senses were heightened as she allowed her eyes to focus once again to the engulfing darkness. This floor was a corridor surrounded by doors, and Donatella could tell by looking through the first door it was a corridor of classrooms. From the looks of the video, Bree didn't appear to be in a classroom of any sort, but it was

Driftwood Springs

impossible to discern with what little information she was able to glean. Donatella turned the door – locked. She quickly proceeded to the next door – locked. She raced to the third door and before she could turn the handle to test the door, the handled turned and the door exploded outward, knocking her to the ground.

With her momentum carrying her backward, Agent Dabria continued into a backward roll, rotating her feet past her torso. Bending her elbows ninety degrees so that the palm of her hands would land flat on the ground, she extended both arms, springing herself into the air and landing on her feet in a near-crouch. The operative from The Syndicate wasted no time and minced no words.

He quickly charged Donatella's crouching form, bringing his right knee up toward Donatella face with blinding speed. Donatella, sensing the action more than seeing the knee, brought both hands up in self-defense. Her hands caught the brunt of the force, and she was able to divert the angle of the knee three-inches past her right cheekbone.

The operative planted his right foot, pivoted while lowering into a crouch of his own, and swept his left foot into Donatella's left leg, knocking her to the ground.

Stay off the ground, she reminded herself as she began to tumble. She rolled onto her left shoulder, feeling the pain return from the knife wound she suffered only two days prior. A loud boom of thunder cracked, followed by an elongated flash of lightning that illuminated the corridor.

"Twenty-six minutes and twenty-five seconds remaining," Donatella heard Buckley mocking as she simultaneously saw her attacker on the prowl once again. *I don't have time for this fight to continue in this manner.*

With the light afforded by the lightning strike, Donatella noticed all the weight of her attacker was on his right leg as he cocked back with his left fist to deliver a vicious blow. Wasting no time of her own, she formed all the energy into her right forearm she could muster and with cobra-like quickness her fist drove into his knee. She heard the audible crack of bone as the hyper extended joint flexed inwardly. The blow that was meant to connect with Donatella's face lost all steam, as her attacker yelled out in shear agony and crumbled to the ground.

Her assailant cradled his malformed knee with both hands as he writhed in pain. *This man will surely be out of the fight*, Donatella thought as she pushed herself to her feet.

"Nice counter-move Agent Dabria, bravo! I had no clue you could go so medieval. But tick-tock, you better get moving. Your hostages are waiting on you to save the day."

Donatella looked into the room that her assailant burst from to find it contained only some desk and chairs. She made her way to the next two doors in sequence, and each one told the same story – locked. When she approached the last door in the corridor, it was unlocked. From underneath the door she could see light and movement. She cautiously turned the knob and pushed the door open.

Once inside she realized that the light was accompanied by sound. It was a sound she was all too familiar with.

"Happy birthday to you. Happy birthday to you. Happy birthday dear Donatella, happy birthday to you. Blow out the candles, my sweet girl and make a wish." Donatella watched her six-year-old self close her eyes and blow out the candles. "Now don't tell anyone your wish or it will not come true," her mom said, glowing with a smile. Donatella remembered this birthday well and the wish she made. *Let this moment last forever.*

She took a step toward the screen that was now paused with her mom's smile frozen on her face. Her beautiful brown eyes felt as if they had embraced Donatella in a hug and would not let her go.

"Twenty-four minutes and fifteen seconds. I suggest you get moving, unless you're prepared for old mommy dear to meet you, your Goddaughter, and poor Mr. Grandson in Twenty-four minutes and five, four, three."

The words and harsh reality broke Donatella from her trance. "I love you mom," she whispered under her breath as she retreated to the door while simultaneously thinking, *I will find who did this and kill them all, starting with Terri Buckley.*

Agent Dabria entered the stairwell and began to jog up the flight of stairs to the 3rd floor. Her left shoulder was now shooting daggers of pain that she instinctively reached up to rub with her right hand. *I was on defense too long during that confrontation. I need to move more expediently,* she thought. She took a deep breath and drew her mental focus from within to face what lay ahead. She pulled open the door and prepared for the impending battle.

The layout of this floor was vastly different from that of the one on the 2nd floor. Whereas the 2nd floor was filled with lecture-style classrooms, this floor sported an open-floor concept that was more rounded than square. Similar to the atrium, this floor was filled with projector screens that circled the entire circumference of the room. On the floor there were a number of workspaces with dual monitors and laptop docking stations. A number of self-serve vending machines were located towards the far left-hand side of this expansive space. The room, set with numerous floor-to-ceiling windows, would emit a tremendous amount of sunlight during the day. However, the only things visible through the windows were the torrential downpour pounding the city and a periodic flash of lightning dancing behind with clouds in the sky.

Donatella cautiously but expediently made her way through what she considered to be a common area. Once she reached the middle of the room, she heard the door across the room groan on its hinges as it was pulled open. Through the door came a short, squirrelly-looking man. He carried in his hand an eighteen-inch baton similar to the retractable one Donatella left downstairs.

Before the door found its resting position within the doorjamb, the hinges groaned once more and a tall, 6-foot, 2-inch, athletic woman stepped into the room. She too carried a baton. A look of abhorrent contorted the sunken cheekbones of her face. She stood next to the man, and had it not been for the dire situation in which she faced this odd pairing of individuals would have been comical.

Donatella could sense the looming clock directly beneath her ticking away relentlessly, and she felt she had limited time to formulate a plan of attack. Taking them both on at the same time would spell her doom, but she would need to dispose of them as quickly as possible. Her plan of attack would start with the man. She had the length on him, whereas she and the woman were of similar stature. She quickly surveyed her surroundings and disconnected one of the power cords connecting the monitor to the electrical outlet. It was the best she could do at the moment, and it would have to be enough.

To her surprise, the man took a step back, while the

woman simultaneously took a step forward. Looked like her plan of attack would need to be altered. The pair began their advance and Donatella advanced too, sticking to her attack-first mindset. As the trio neared each other, the woman fanned to her left and the man fanned to her right. This move simplified Donatella's attack vectors, as she kicked one of the chairs and sent it careening towards the woman, knocking her off her stride as she diverted her path to the right to focus on the man.

He raised his right hand, brandishing the baton back above his head and swung it in a quick arc toward Donatella. She pulled up short, and this allowed the baton to miss her by mere inches. She could feel the wind from the force of the swing as the baton traveled past her face. She jabbed forward with the cord and yanked it back with a snap connecting with the forehead of the man, staggering him for the moment Donatella needed. She followed this with a right knee to his groin and a jump punch that connected with his jaw.

Donatella felt more than saw the blow to her left ribs that buckled her in momentary pain. The woman was back in the fight. As the woman prepared for her second blow, Donatella lashed out with the cord, as if she was throwing a right hook at the woman. Satisfyingly it connected with the left side of the woman's face, slowing down the velocity of the baton as it connected again with Donatella's left ribs. Attention fully focused on this new threat, Donatella quickly wrapped the cord across her knuckles. The cord, while a nice deterrent from afar, took too long to reach its intended target. Having it wrapped snugly across her fist would serve as the best weapon she could muster.

Donatella knew the man, who she could see from the

corner of her eye beginning to gain his footing again, would be back in this fight soon enough. Lightning once again came calling in the background, followed by its partner in this dance that lit up the second-floor battle arena. The woman, sticking with her weapon of choice and not deviating in her plan, prepared to swing again. Donatella, the quicker of the two, jabbed the woman with her left hand. Once, twice, three time with the third blow sending pain through her left shoulder once again.

Switching tactics and launch angles, Donatella crouched to generate force through her legs and with her left leg she kicked the exposed right side of the woman's torso, connecting with her ribs. Where Donatella had more cushion to absorb the blows the woman dealt out, the other woman was more skin and bones. Donatella wasn't sure, but she could have sworn she felt a rib snap, and from the reaction of the woman she was confident in this assertion.

The woman dropped the baton as she reached for her now-throbbing side. Without hesitation, Donatella reached down with her left hand and retrieved the baton that lay rolling across the ground. As the man approached from Donatella's right side, she performed a reverse pivot and with a backhand, smashed the baton into his face. She tossed the baton from her left hand to her dominate right hand. With the cord still wrapped around her knuckles, awaiting further use, holding the baton became tricky as she could not fully sense the handle in her hand. However, she had enough of the sensation to realize it was planted firmly and would suffice for the moment.

Donatella allowed the baton to fall beneath her waist, slightly behind her thigh. She dipped her right shoulder, and with all her strength she swung the baton in an uppercut motion and connected underneath the male assailant's chin. This blow knocked him off of his feet, and Donatella hoped this would knock him out of this fight, but she was unsure as a blow to the back of her neck sent her sprawling across the floor.

The woman had gained her second wind and was obviously pissed at the turn this fight had taken. The PA crackled, "Eighteen minutes and twenty-four seconds. I highly suggest you get a move on before the entire building goes boom!"

Donatella gritted her teeth and forced her way back to her feet. She shook her head a couple of times to loosen the cobwebs and regain focus. With time stacked against her she once again decided to press the attack.

Moving with the grace of a swan and the quickness of a cheetah, Donatella swung the baton at the woman's head. The woman raised her left arm in defense, a move Donatella anticipated. Before she made contact with the woman's arm, Donatella redirected the arc of the swing and connected with the left side of her torso, breaking another rib. As the baton bounced from the contact Donatella quickly switched to a backhand grip and smashed the baton against the woman's right side. The woman, now in severe pain from at minimum one broken rib and likely several, hunched over to protect her midsection. Sensing the end was near, Donatella bounced the baton off of the back of the woman's head, rendering her unconscious before her limp form flattened on the ground.

Donatella quickly surveyed the room for any remaining threats. The uppercut blow she administered to the man had knocked him out as well. Donatella unwrapped the cord from her hand and let it drop to the floor, but she would carry the baton forward. As she maneuvered her way through the remainder of the open space, the screen above her exit came to life. The picture that graced the screen was a picture of her mom and her dad holding hands as they boarded a white private yacht. The picture stopped her in her tracks as the video began to play, as she had never seen this video footage before.

The two walked across the plank leading to the entrance of the vessel. They were both smiling, carefree and without any premonition that this would be their last moment on Earth. Donatella knew how this story ended and knew she needed to press forward, but there she stood, frozen. She was captivated in a trance-like state that gripped her limbs and rendered fighting its hold useless.

Once the couple moved out of site of the camera, the screen changed to an aerial view looking down on the boat. Donatella tightened her grip around the handle of the baton as she braced for what she knew would come next. A fireball erupted, engulfing the private yacht in a sea of red and blue flames. Donatella felt a tear slide over her cheek and down to her chin. The tear hung precariously at the end of her chin until it permeated through the darkness and eventually splashed on the marble floor.

"I know it's hard to watch," came the voice from Terri Buckley. "If my parents had been incinerated in a fireball like that, I would be mad at the world. I would want vengeance on those responsible. I would stop at nothing until I obtained that vengeance. Sadly, for you, Agent Dabria, you will not have the chance to enact your revenge, because in fifteen minutes you'll suffer the same fate as dear old mom and dad."

Donatella, hatred coursing through her veins, kicked

open the door and proceeded up the final flight of stairs to the fourth floor. *Bree, I will save you! Last stop and you will be safe.* She pulled herself up the stairs, reaching the door to the fourth and final floor. She turned the handle down, pulled open the door, and walked in.

This floor unlike the previous three had no clear definition. In fact, it was an open space that had not yet begun the trim work exhibited on the other floors. On the far end of the floor, Donatella could make out the outline of a person sitting in a chair. However, in the immediate foreground stood there was an adversary she would need to defeat in order to save Bree.

Donatella strode with a renewed purpose as she was fifty yards and one impediment from achieving her goal. She wasn't sure what she would do about the journalist, but before she could ponder that thought, she needed to rescue Bree.

Donatella's adversary stalked towards her with ever-increasing speed that turned into a slight jog. Donatella picked up her pace as well. When the two were ten feet apart Donatella brought the baton up and swung towards her attacker. With lightening quick speed, the assailant caught the baton in his left hand and kicked Donatella in the gut with his right foot. The force of the kick sent Donatella tumbling backwards, head of over heels until she slid to a stop ten yards from where she started. The brute, who she could now clearly see, was massive, muscular, and quicker than she had expected. He looked down at Donatella with a smirk, still holding the baton in his hand. He took it with both hands and snapped it like a twig. He tossed away both pieces and motioned for Donatella to press her attack once again.

She stood to her feet, dusted herself off, and thought of her best plan of attack against a foe who was superior in size and strength and from what she could tell as quick as she was. Again, the brute extended his arm, turned his palm skyward, and curled his fingers back and forth in the universal sign of "come get it."

Donatella pounced from her stance at this massive human being. Immediately she swung her right fist for his face, which he brushed away as if shooing away a pesky fly. She countered with a jab toward his throat with her left hand to which he shrugged his shoulder and dropping his chin protecting the neck. Her blow landed on his chin but had no effect. Continuing to press, she kicked her right leg towards his midsection. He trapped her leg between his body and his left arm. He reached across his body with his right arm grasping her leg between both hands. He started a 360-degree turn that pulled Donatella from her feet. After two full spins he released his grasp on Donatella, catapulting her into the air. She flew roughly fifteen yards before she hit the ground with a resounding thud.

The weather outside Building 1 of the Orbitz Technology Campus seemed to be nearing its crescendo. The rain now coming down in sheets was accompanied by the rhythmic base from the thunder and the well-timed flash of lightning. In her rage and desire to stay on the offensive, she had forgone the years of training she received from her Krav Maga sensei, Master Yoshida.

She lay there on the ground, eyes closed while thinking back to the numerous hand-to-hand sparring sessions the two of them had gone through during her time as his pupil and disciple. She thought back to the countless times she lost those hand-to-hand sessions and her drive to get better.

She thought back to the time in which she finally bested him. Her focus during that confrontation was letting her defense transform into her lethal counter attacks. In admiration of his student's success, he bowed to her first, showing the respect he had gained for her and her abilities.

With clarity of mind and a narrowing sharpness of her eyes, Donatella stood firm on her two feet, straightening the hem of her shirt with a tug and smiling. Her assailant cocked his head to the side. She straightened her arm, turned her palm to the sky and with the similar mocking motion, flexed her fingers forward and backwards summoning her opponent toward her.

A smile of superiority spread across his facial features, thinking he clearly held the upper hand. Without hesitation, he approached his prey now on the attack and looking to end this fight.

The beast swung with his right-hand, which Donatella caught in the air, grabbing him at the wrist with her left hand. This set her shoulder on fire, but she ignored the pain. She shot her right hand to the right side of her assailant's neck pushing his head to the left. Taking a step forward with her left leg, she exploded her knee into his solar plexus, while simultaneously reaching behind his neck and pulling him forward. Releasing his neck and connecting a blow from her right fist to his left jaw, she released his right wrist in time to catch his face as it careened toward her now-free left hand. She crossed her body with her right hand, grabbing the underside of his neck and violently rotating his neck skyward. It forced his body to rotate 270 degrees, landing him on his right side.

Down but certainly not out. She grabbed his left arm by the wrist before it could fall to his side, rotating it enough to complete his full revolution that landed him on his face. She hyper-extended the arm with his wrist pointing back toward his shoulder, she exploded her knee through the elbow shattering both the humerus and the radius bones in his left arm, and she discarded the limb as he had previously done with the two pieces of the baton.

Her adversary bellowed out in both the realization of being bested and his body going into shock. However, his cries were cut short as Donatella drove her knee into the top of his spinal column, and his world went dark.

Donatella paused there, knee in the crevice between his head and shoulder, breathing heavily. She had given what energy she had left into this battle, and her body was now losing some adrenaline and edge.

"Bravo, killer! As I said before, I knew you had it in you! But tick-tock! You have not reached your destination, and the clock still ticks. You now have nine minutes and three seconds."

Bruised and nearly out on her feet, Donatella began to run to the slumped-over figure of Bree. Thirty yards to go, twenty yards to go – *something isn't right*, she thought as she approached the figure. At ten yards, her heart nearly stopped. She raced around to the front and there sitting in front of her was Sal Grandson. She dropped to her knees in abject devastation.

"YOU LIED!" she yelled at the top of her lungs. "You wretched lying bitch!"

"Me? I didn't lie!" countered Buckley innocently. "I told you Sal was to the right and your precious Goddaughter was to the left. I see how you can be confused, your left was my right and your right was my left. Honest mistake, I assure you. And to prove I am a woman of my word, I will disarm the C4 to Sal Grandson's chair."

Donatella had not noticed the beeping of the timer until the sound stopped emanating through the room. Donatella retrieved the knife sitting on the floor next to Grandson and began to saw through his bindings.

"I also promised I would give you ten more minutes once you rescued a hostage and I disarmed the bomb. Doing so would provide you the opportunity to rescue the second hostage. And with that you now have 18 minutes and 30 seconds. But I also made you another promise. You will not save them both and should you try, you will die in that attempt." The coldness had returned to her voice. Donatella freed both of Sal's hands, removed his gag, and handed him the knife so he could continue to cut through his leg bindings.

"I'm sorry, Donatella!" Sal said.

Business-like and detached, Donatella responded, "My car is about thirty meters outside of the campus. The door is unlocked and inside the glove box you will find a phone. Call the police department and let them know what is happening here. I need to go and save Bree."

She stood, not waiting on his response and ran toward the door.

"Brava!" came the voice from Buckley. "You have chosen to die here tonight."

19

FRIDAY, SEPTEMBER 20TH – 11:30 P.M
ORBITZ TECHNOLOGY CAMPUS

Donatella ran, arms pumping and legs moving her as fast as they could, though she willed them to go faster. The blood in her ears racing as the mocking words from Buckley replayed in her mind, "You cannot save them both – You will not save them both." As the words haunted her, she pumped her arms faster. She burst through the stairwell door on the fourth floor and rapidly made her decent, opting to jump down the set of stairs instead of hitting them one at a time.

She yanked open the door for the third floor and was greeted with the still picture of the exploding boat now visible on all screens circling the room. The image of the fireball on each of the screen provided enough ambient light to see additional features of the room. Donatella noticed both the man and the woman still unconscious where she left them during their battle. As she weaved her way through the voluminous room, Buckley's voice taunted once more, "...you'll suffer the same fate as dear old mom and dad." Donatella pushed harder, ignoring the pain in her left shoulder and tapping further into her energy reserves to propel her forward faster. Without slowing down, she plowed through the stairwell door on the third floor, and in similar fashion leapt down each set of stairs to minimize her time in the stairwell.

She pulled open the door to the second floor, and she could hear the serenades all over again coming from now the hall's first room. "Happy birthday to you. Happy birthday to you. Happy birthday, dear Donatella. Happy birthday to you. Blow out the candles my sweet girl and make a wish." She ignored the words as they trailed off behind her and she continued down the hallway.

The man, her first assailant still lay writhing in pain on the floor. Donatella was surprised he had not gone completely into shock. Upon hearing the door open and footsteps approaching, he momentarily looked up, and Donatella kicked him square in the face without skipping a beat. Probably unnecessary since he was out of the fight, but Donatella needed to let off a bit of steam. Furthermore, Sal would need to come this same direction, and she didn't want him dealing with this murderous bastard. Reaching the second-floor stairwell door, she exploded through this obstacle and proceeded down the stairs. As she traversed the final flight, Donatella was still wrestling with a decision. A decision she was 95% sure she would need to make, but one she hoped she wouldn't regret.

As she hit the ground level, she pulled open the door and ran past the bank of elevators and back through the electric turnstile. She looked up at the clock within the atrium of Orbitz Technology Campus's Building 1. The ominous red glow of the clock read 15:00 and quickly flipped to 14:59. For Donatella the decision was solidified. She stopped in the middle of the floor, picked up her utility belt, strapped it around her waist and headed for the electric turnstile located on the right side of the building. As she ran through an audible chime rang loudly. Donatella looked back over her shoulder at the clock, which now read 9:47.

Donatella understood the dynamics she now needed to encounter. Hand-to-hand combat, especially in her current state, could not be achieved in fifteen minutes. Losing the five minutes from grabbing her utility belt also meant she needed to dispose of her adversary quickly, or at a minimum blast her way through as she made her way to the other side of each floor. Though this plan was not ideal, it was the best one she had, and she didn't have the time or the energy to think of another one. So, she pressed forward. As she headed for the back stairwell, Buckley's voice made a predictable appearance.

"My, my. We must be getting desperate. Opting to go with your assortment of weapons in lieu of keeping five minutes. I hope for your sake and the sake of Bree this gamble pays off. Time will tell, that's for sure. But you have to ask yourself, had you shaved those five minutes off in the beginning, would you be better off than you are now? Oh, how the decisions we make come back to bite us in the ass. But I must warn you, since you've upped the ante, my team will do the same. Good luck – you'll need it!"

Donatella finished climbing the first flight of stairs on the right side of Building 1. She quickly pulled the magazine from her Sig Sauer pistol, verified she had the full complement of fifteen 9 mm bullets, and reinserted the magazine back into the gun. She had fired three rounds into Sal's door and vaguely recalled swapping the partially spent magazine with a fresh one, but she was not leaving anything to chance. Considering the varying layouts on the other side of the building, Donatella figured she could expect the same on this side, and she would need to survey her surroundings on the spot. Her plan was simple, if there is cover on the direct path from one side of the floor to the other, she would take a momentary pause to quickly survey the remainder of her path. If there was not any cover, she would shoot anything moving. She was certain anything moving in this building on this night was a foe, and she didn't have time to discern any differences. She took one final deep breath and rushed through the door.

Gun at the ready, right hand on the butt of the gun and left-hand cradling the right, she quickly searched out the exit sign, thus leading to the next set of stairs. In her quick assessment she could see the floor split off into three distinct paths. The one in the middle had a set of double doors that presumably continued down the main path of the floor. The path to the right appeared to hold a set of computer labs, and the path to the left appeared to hold offices. Though the floor was separated into these three distinct sections, the walls on the floor were made of transparent glass.

Surveying from left to right, eyes trained over the metal gun sights, Donatella moved at a rapid pace to the double door straight ahead. As she reached for the handle of the door, a bullet came whizzing by her right ear, shattering the glass in front of her. Donatella crouched and stepped through the jagged frame of the door being careful not to cut any appendages as she moved. Two more shots rang out, one flying harmlessly through the empty frame and the other making impact with the glass within the other window. The shower of broken glass exploded around Donatella, sending shards in several different directions. One of the glass fragments sliced open a shallow gash on the top half of Donatella's right hand. She could discern that the shots were coming from behind her current location, but she didn't have eyes on the perpetrator.

She blindly fired two shots over her left shoulder as she began running away from the incoming flurry of bullets. Three more bullets followed in her wake, as Donatella slid to the ground and sought refuge behind a rectangular office desk. The clock was ticking, and she didn't have time for this cat-and-mouse game she felt creeping its way into this confrontation. She spotted the exit sign, and a plan hastily materialized in her mind.

She rose to a crouch and fired off two more shots in the direction she felt the incoming bullets had originated from. Once the last 9 mm shell casing ejected from her pistol, Donatella jumped into a full sprint toward the exit. It took a moment for the return volley to begin, but once it did the gun seemed to be on full auto. All doors leading to the stairwells up to this moment pushed into the stairwell and she prayed this one would be no different.

She heard the crunch of glass from behind her as the assailant gave chase, spraying wildly. The sound of semi-automatic gunfire mixed with the shattering of glass in this enclosed space was maddening, but Donatella pushed forward. Either the assailant realized that she was headed for the door or his erratic gunfire impacted the door on accident. Regardless of the reason, Donatella ducked as she forced her way through the door.

Instead of immediately bolting up the stairwell to the

third floor, Donatella slammed the door closed, maneuvered her way behind the door, pushed against the wall, and made herself as small as possible. She placed her foot slightly in front of her body so that when the door slammed open, her foot and not her face would take the force of the door. Five seconds later, the door came flying open and the hunter became her prey.

Donatella pushed the door away from her body in time to see a man roughly 6-foot even bounding up the stairs. She aimed the gun at the necessary angle and elevation and fired two more shots. Each 9 mm hit true in the back of her assailant's head and his body immediately fell limp to the ground. Wasting no time, Donatella ran toward the steps, hurdled the body as gravity pulled it back down the stairs, and made her way to the third floor.

Donatella could feel her heart pounding against her rib cage, but she knew she needed to press on. She had to do everything in her power to save Bree. She had no intention of letting her die – not here – not tonight.

Over the PA system, Buckley chimed in, "Well done! Did the FBI teach you how to shoot people from behind? I don't recall reading that in the handbook as proper operating procedure. Regardless, you have seven minutes before the whole right side of Building 1 suffers the same fate as the yacht your parents boarded so many years ago. Be sure to tell them, dear mom and dad, 'hi' for me when you see them."

Agent Dabria brushed aside the comment and focused on the task at hand. She needed to ascend two more flights, clear two more floors, and take on an unspecified number of bad actors in her theater. To this point she had managed to successfully navigate each encounter, but they were not as clean as she would have liked. She glanced down at her hand to see the cut. Though superficial, it was still bleeding. The blood began to make is way down her right hand and onto her palm, making the grip on the pistol slick and more tenuous. With less than seven minutes remaining, she flung the door open, bolted into the room, and immediately took a turn to her right.

A hail of bullets pelted the plaster in the hallway and eventually the door as it swung shut. Agent Dabria spotted the muzzle flashes – three from what she could tell. The gamble to divert her path to the right versus her direct nature each previous time had saved her life. With nine bullets remaining in her clip, she leveled the gun and squeezed the trigger.

Bang! Bang!

Two shots in rapid succession. The muzzle flashes closest to Donatella immediately ceased. Before she could refocus her aim, the other two realized the shots were coming from a different angle in the room, and they began to spray bullets in her direction. Donatella ran against the wall, a dangerous notion, and she had no time to survey the room. She took in as much as she could while running at top speed. With the trail of bullets tracing her steps growing ever closer, Donatella dove to the ground just as the bullets raced overhead. She was three feet from an aisle that ran perpendicular to the wall she had been running against.

She swiftly crawled on her hands and knees to the opening as the trajectory of the bullets began to home in on her location. As she crawled, the guns stopped firing as the two remaining members of the team switched their tactics.

Donatella knew being outnumbered in a gunfight, especially if the remaining members had split up, which is what she figured they had done, could end badly for her. She holstered her Sig Sauer semi-automatic pistol and retrieved three of her throwing knives from her scabbard. She placed one in the left cuff of her jacket while securing the other two in either hand as she crawled.

The lifeless sound engulfing the room into a silent bubble had Donatella straining her ears for any sound – any movement that would betray the location of her pursuers. She decided to raise her body enough to see over the aisle she found herself traveling. She lifted her body with a slow urgency as the clock was ticking and time was running out. She did not see either assailant immediately in front of her. She quickly and quietly preformed a ninety-degree turn left, back toward the direction she came from, and spotted one of the men moving in the direction of the wall. She raised her right hand and let fly one of her twelve Japanese Shinobi throwing knives.

She watched as the gleam of silver streaked through the room seeking its target. The point of the metal hit home in the side of his neck as the blade continued to pierce the skin to the edge of the blade. The man began to gargle blood, but Donatella was already on the move. She knew with a detached certainty that he was dead and that his partner would hear his death rattle in the stillness of the night.

She crouched as she moved, staying level with the top of the aisle as she searched for the remaining attacker. Realizing she was running out of time, she decided to make her dash toward the door. Donatella stood and ran down the remaining length of the aisle and turned down the main walkway. As she did, she saw her last impediment standing at the door with his eyes on his sights. She immediately threw herself to the ground while simultaneously flinging her throwing knife from her left hand. The bullets momentarily occupied the space she voided as they continued to fly toward the back of the room.

Donatella hit the ground thinking, T*his is it. Nowhere to hide.* But her instincts refused to let her give in. She reached down to her hip, pulling her Sig Sauer from its holster while preforming a log roll to her left as quickly as she could. The impacts of the bullets tore chunks out of the marble as she rolled doing her best to avoid the incoming blast. Gun in hand and now laying prone, she fired off the remaining seven shots from her gun's magazine. A shot from the attacker tore into her right hip, and she let out a primordial yell.

Time slowed perceptively, and the room was once again silent. Donatella waited for the final shot to fire that would end her life. In that split moment she felt her heart sink as she had officially failed Bree, failed her parents. The Syndicate was going to win. However, three seconds passed, and no shot was sent her direction. She looked up, slide on the gun retracted in perpetuity from the last bullet leaving the chamber, to see the last member of this trio sitting slumped at the door on the floor.

She laid her head on the cool marble, stunned into disbelief.

"Impressive!" projected the voice from the PA system. "I have to say, I pretty much figured you were done for and yet nine-lives Dabria pulls out another one. How is that pesky wound to the leg? Will it hamper the remainder of your journey to save your sweet, precious Goddaughter? It would be a shame to come this far and fall short. But alas, it seems that's exactly what will happen. You have three minutes and fifteen seconds remaining."

Donatella pushed herself to her feet ignoring the throbbing in her shoulder, the blood still trickling from her hand and the new impediment to her leg. She flexed her thigh quickly and realized she was still good to proceed. Adrenaline and the foreboding that she would save Bree blocked all pain sensors, and she tore into a full sprint. The first plant of her right foot shot pain up her right side, but she ignored it and pushed through the door. Unable to bound two steps at once this time, she quickly hit each step, teeth gritting each time she pushed off of her right leg. At the top, the fourth floor of Building 1 of the new Orbitz Technology Campus, Donatella pulled open the door and stepped in.

Once inside, Donatella noticed the red glow of the countdown clock directly in front of her and in front of Bree. Bree's back was to Donatella with her face to the clock forced to watch the clock countdown her pending doom. Before Donatella could rush to her aide, she was tackled by an unseen assailant, falling to the ground with the assailant landing on top of her. The attacker, a woman, began to pelt Donatella with one head shot after another. The fourth blow caused Donatella to see stars, just after she managed to push the woman off of her. She stole a glance at the clock. 2:10. Donatella pondered quickly, *if I make it to Bree, will the clock stop or do I need to dispose of this foe first?* Figuring she knew the answer, she attacked. She felt lighter and realized that in the skirmish the woman had loosened her utility belt, which was now on the ground next to her.

Undeterred, she limped forward and threw a tired punch at the woman that missed wildly. The woman punched Donatella in the head, nearly rendering her unconscious. As her head snapped back and to the side, the ominous red glare spoke its silent warning, 1:36. Donatella's mind raced and again presented a similar solution, the best offense was sometimes defense.

Donatella, running on fumes, squeezed the last drop of energy from her reserves. The woman reared back and swung once again at Donatella's face. Donatella shot her left arm up, still throbbing in pain, to block the blow from the attacker. As she swiped the blow outward and to the left of her body, she grasped the forearm of the assailant in a death grip. She quickly shot out her right hand and grasped the left forearm of the attacker. Holding both arms in a vice grip at 45-degree angles to the ground, Donatella took two quick minute steps back, right leg first –pain radiating—followed by the left leg. Once the heel of her left foot planted on the ground with savage speed, Donatella kicked her foot upward, planting the heel of her right foot into the chin of the attacker.

The brutality and speed of the kick snapped the head back of the assailant. Donatella released her arms and both women folded to the ground. Physically and mentally spent, Donatella eyed the clock, 56 seconds remaining. She began to army-crawl toward Bree. Her left shoulder was barely able to take her lumbering weight and her right leg grew stiffer by the moment. But she crawled.

She crawled because this would not be how things ended for her. She crawled because she was resigned to the fact Bree would not die here tonight. She crawled because she had unfinished work to do. But most importantly she crawled for the memory of her parents. For their last moments on Earth. For the pain she still needed to dole out

– severe and unrelenting punishment to the outfit calling themselves The Syndicate.

She reached Bree's chair, and from her prone vantage point she could see the C4 under the chair and the arming light lit. She looked up. 15 seconds on the clock.

"Turn off your damn bomb!" she exclaimed. "Damn it, Buckley. Turn it off." The light persisted. 7, 6, 5. "Bree, I'm sorry love." 3, 2 – Donatella shut her eyes, awaiting the inevitable.

And then – nothing. Donatella looked at the C4 under the chair and the arming light was now dull and the countdown clock had stopped :02. A sense of utter relief overcame Donatella as she forced herself to one knee. Bree's bindings had been tied into handcuff knots behind her back. Donatella made quick work of the knots and stood to face Bree. She looked down at her Goddaughter, and her Goddaughter looked back at her. Eyes still wide from the flurry of activity, Donatella removed the gag from her mouth.

"LOOKOUT!" she shouted. Donatella pivoted to an unknown force her Goddaughter had discovered, but it was too late. A gunshot rang out and the force from the bullet finished spinning Donatella around, knocking her to the ground where she landed on her back.

20

FRIDAY, SEPTEMBER 20TH – 11:45 P.M
ORBITZ TECHNOLOGY CAMPUS

Donatella lay motionless on her back, staring into the ceiling. Blood was now pouring from her left shoulder as it had now been introduced to a new pain sensation. Try as she might, Donatella found it nearly impossible to move any muscle in her body. She began to ponder how she was shot. She incapacitated all the foes she had encountered. However, the direction from where the gun was fired signified the unknown assailant was also in the room when she arrived.

She pulled visuals from her mind's eye that she subconsciously processed when she entered the room. She saw the red glow of the clock, Bree sitting in the chair watching the clock. Or was she watching the clock? Donatella reached deeper into her memory bank to replay and freeze that moment. *No, she wasn't looking at the clock. The clock was above her head, and she was looking straight ahead in front of her. Almost directly in front, her head was tilted slightly to the left.*

Donatella shifted her eyes to the left as she stared at the

still picture from her memory. *There was an office to the left. How did I miss it?* She mentally kicked herself for this foolish blunder.

"Special Agent Donatella Dabria!" the voice of Terri Buckley powered through the PA with a real-time 3D sound. So nice to see you again, and in-person nonetheless."

Donatella's eyes shot open, regaining a small sense of focus. *In person?* She heard the PA system thud as the microphone fell, and Terri Buckley kicked Donatella in her exposed left ribs. Buckley dragged Donatella until her limp form was laid out in front of Bree. Buckley elevated her to a seated position and leaned her against Bree's legs, which were still bound to the chair.

"There you go," Buckley said as Donatella's form slouched against Bree's legs. Buckley took a couple of steps back, one so Donatella could get a good look at her, and two because she still didn't trust the woman.

As Buckley prepared to speak, lightning lit up the skyline through the window at Buckley's back.

"I have to say, you are one hard lady to kill. Much harder than your parents for sure. Admittedly, I thought you would have died on your first ascent of the building. Sure, everyone knows how good 'Special Agent Dabria' is in the field, but you impressed me. So much so that I had to travel onsite to see it for myself. And I will say, you put on one hell of a show. So, to that I must give you a round of applause."

Buckley tucked the gun under her left arm and gave Donatella an almost genuine round of applause.

"But I told you several times," eyes narrowing and the menace deep in her voice. "You cannot save them both. You will not save them both. And if you tried, you would die trying."

The lightning flashed again along with the thunder on a rhythmic, evenly spaced timing.

"The decision had been made prior to you entering this building that Bree was going to die. Either you would fail making your way up the left side, in which case I would have allowed the entire building to explode."

Lightning lit up the sky once again behind Buckley.

"You would have saved Sal Grandson, which you did – so there's a check in the win column for you. Because let's face it, you were predetermined to go to your left with the picture of your Goddaughter perfectly aligned on the left side of the atrium. Oh, and I may have had some help in that arena as well. But no need to harp on that. In saving Sal, you would have died on the inevitable self-righteous duty you have to save your Bree. You surely should have died at the hands of The Syndicate operatives; they are such a disappointment. Bree would have still been blown up, and Sal Grandson would have been alive to write a nice internet article about it. An inside scoop with a firsthand eye-witness account."

The downpour of the rain continued in the background and the lightning tickled the sky once again.

"But no!" she said, waving the gun in the direction of Donatella and Bree. "You made it to the top and ruined my carefully crafted plan. So, I'm here to improvise. Please understand, you are not leaving here alive, and frankly neither is Bree. While my preference was for you to die in a fiery inferno like your parents, a bullet between your eyes, and a bullet between the eyes of this twerp will still do the job. And for kicks, I'll still detonate the C4, leveling this entire structure."

As she spoke, Donatella was processing information and formulating a plan. Although Buckley was cloaked in the room's darkness, her body came into full view with each lightning strike. A strike that took place every twelve seconds. *Now,* Dabria thought.

The sky lit up once again, fully illuminating the room on the fourth floor.

"After I'm done with you and Bree, I plan to pay a visit to her mommy and her daddy. My goal is to rid this Earth of everyone you ever cared about or who has cared about you. You need to understand there are consequences when you interfere with the life and livelihood of others. You can take it to your grave knowing that I will keep my promise, as I have kept them here today."

Donatella finished the counting in her head, *10, 11.* Ignoring the pulsating pain and blood spurting from her left shoulder, she quickly pulled her left arm above her head, at the same time bringing up her right hand. She reached into the cuff of her left sleeve and extracted the Japanese Shinobi throwing knife she stored there while crawling on the ground between the aisle during the gun battle. The room lit up from the lightning strike outside as her internal count hit 12. She hurled the knife across the room toward Buckley, who was too shocked to respond.

Once the knife left her hand, Donatella leaped to her feet. In her state she knew the odds of hitting anything vital would be a stretch, but if she could just manage to both wound and distract her long enough, she could end this once and for all. The throwing knife sliced into the right arm of Buckley as she instinctively raised her hand to fend off an incoming threat. Realizing what happened, Buckley began to swing the gun in the direction of Agent Dabria – but it was too late. Before Buckley could apply the pressure needed to pull the trigger back on the gun, Donatella performed a two-leg dropkick into her torso.

The force of the kick catapulted Buckley into the semi-finished window behind her. The window shattered, and Buckley's momentum carried her through the window while gravity sucked her down to the Earth.

Donatella landed on her back and groaned with pain. With that last burst of energy, Donatella was spent. *I need to make sure this is truly over,* she thought. She clawed at the ground to find purchase and push herself to a seated position. She rotated her feet back toward Bree and then laid down on her stomach. Her shoulder was once again on fire and pouring blood. Her right leg was now completely numb and non-responsive. She once again army-crawled, this time using nothing but her upper body strength. She grimaced with each movement, and after a few moments she reached the edge. The rain flowing horizontally through the window pelted her face and provided a cooling sensation. She looked over the area directly below the broken window in search of a fallen form. The lightning illuminated the sky once again and there, laying atop the tarps Donatella had noticed during her reconnaissance of the building, was the sprawled body of Terri Buckley – and then the scene went dark. In the backdrop she could hear sirens approaching.

Good, Sal was able to make it so safety, she thought before her world went dark.

EPILOGUE
THOMPSON RESIDENCE (1812 GARDEN STREET)

Three weeks had passed since the confrontation at the Orbitz Technology Campus, and Donatella Dabria could still feel the effects of what she endured to bring the entire episode to an end. As she sat on the plush sofa, leg elevated on the ottoman, she thought about how close she had come to losing it all, to losing Bree, and to letting her only family, the Hartley's down.

Against her doctors' wishes, Donatella signed herself out of the hospital on Sunday night so that she could travel to New York to sit in on the trial. Jasmyn Thompson, a new friend of sorts took the journey with her, as the doctor demanded she not travel alone if she was insistent on leaving the hospital before her wounds had properly healed. In the eyes of the doctor, his preference was to keep her in the hospital for a week, but he was decisively overruled.

Jasmyn and her husband had been gracious enough to stop in periodically at Donatella's residence to ensure she was healing properly and had everything she needed. On several occasions, similarly to today, they would invite her over, and they would spend some time getting to know one another. This was something she had not done while she worked undercover protecting the Hartley's, but getting to know the Thompson's was something she rather enjoyed.

The Trial of Clarence Carmichael lasted only a week. His sister, Jane, came to the first day of his trial but decided she could not endure the embarrassment her brother had brought to the family. The trial was the buzz of New York, and when Jane refused to report on the trial, the story was handed off to another hungry journalist, and Jane was placed on suspension for insubordination. During her suspension, she spent a couple of days in North Carolina visiting with Sal. Although he played hardball constantly with Jane, underneath she could tell he still had feelings for her.

With the testimony of Frank Hartley and the evidence the FBI was able to secure, Clarence was found guilty and sentenced to twenty years in prison. The Hartley's decided they would not move back to New York, but they also didn't want to live in Driftwood Springs any longer. Many of the neighbors blamed them for the terror that was brought into the neighborhood. In the end, they were relocated to an undisclosed location that only a few people knew about, one of those being Donatella.

The truth about Detective Wilson made a splash on the local news, giving a black eye to the CMPD. The charges of murder were subsequently dropped against Douglass Grant and Diane Dresser. The joint charges brought questions to the involvement of Douglas and Diane with one another, but they stuck to the story that Wilson was looking for anyone to blame and randomly selected them both. While the residents of Driftwood Springs bought the story, Donatella knew the secret they still kept.

"Earth to Donatella," Jasmyn said, pulling her from deep thought.

"I'm sorry. I was just daydreaming," she stated in her old familiar Southern drawl.

"Is it the pain again?" Jasmyn asked. "We can prop your leg up with another pillow if it's giving you any trouble.

"No, I'm okay."

Jasmyn gave her that you-better-not-be-lying-to-me look. "Okay, well if you start to feel any pain, you let us know and we will grab you another pillow"

Donatella nodded her head in acquiescence.

"Marcellous and I called you over for a special reason today. Even though it's only been a few weeks, we wanted to share the news with close friends – we are going to have a baby!" Jasmyn had a smile that stretched from ear to ear.

"I am so happy for you both! Do you know what you are going to have?"

"It's a little too early to tell, but we will be sure to let you know as soon as we find out, because we also would like for you to be our baby's Godmother."

Donatella was rendered speechless.

"We know we've only known you a few weeks, and being a Godmother can come with a load of responsibilities, but we think you would be perfect. Plus, there aren't too many people that Marcellous and I truly trust."

Caught in the moment, Donatella responded, "Yes," and Jasmyn leaned over to squeeze her in a heartfelt embrace. As they hugged, there was still a loose end from three weeks ago that had not tied together nicely. The body of Terri Buckley was never recovered.

READY TO UNLOCK the surprise Terri has in store for Donatella next? Purchase **Hour of Reckoning** and see if she can outwit her former partner.

IF YOU ENJOYED Driftwood Springs and Donatella's endless pursuit to save the children, please consider leaving a **review** so other readers just like you can find this book.

Note from the Author

THANK you for purchasing Driftwood Springs and diving into the world of Special Agent Donatella Dabria. The concept for the novel came to me several years ago with the simple premise; How much do you know about what goes on behind the close doors in your own neighborhood? It can be a scary proposition.

Then I decided to up the ante by introducing the element of children within the neighborhood being abducted. When the children began to disappear, the secrets began to unravel.

Finally, every good mystery needs a hero. Immediately I decided the hero would be a woman and that she would be kick-ass. I have a young daughter whom we teach to be strong, resilient, and sure of herself. With that as my backdrop, I decided the hero should exhibit those same qualities, and thus Donatella was born.

Thank you so much for reading. If you want to stay current about upcoming books, feel free to sign up for my **newsletter**.

SINCERELY,
Demetrius Jackson

Hour of Reckoning Blurb

A TRAIL OF TRAPS. A timetable of death. Can she survive a sinister plot for revenge?

Special Agent Donatella Dabria is always looking over her shoulder. Tormented by the peril her job has put her loved ones in, she's constantly trying to anticipate the ruthless moves of her vindictive rival. So she has no doubt her old enemy is back for blood when taunting clues turn up in a vicious case of adultery turned fatal.

Taking over from the inexperienced cop bungling the investigation, Donatella vows to stop the killer's grisly promise of executing everybody close to her heart. But with the sadist intent on seeing her suffer, the determined fed battles a tragically growing body count...

Can she endure a maze of murders designed to lead her to her end?

Buy *Hour of Reckoning* to wind back a murderous clock today!

Excerpt from Hour of Reckoning

Marcellous Thompson gripped the steering wheel of his royal blue 2018 Tesla Model S as he weaved back and forth through the nighttime traffic. The performance model upgrade and the dual motors provided the torque needed to hurry past any traffic unwilling, or in many cases too slow, to accommodate his rapid rate of speed.

"Damn it, Marcellous. Hurry! This is all your fault! I will not forgive you for this," Jasmyn screamed from the passenger side.

"My fault. My fault? If I recall we were both there and fully engaged in this matter that now has us in this fine predicament."

"Well, if you don't hurry up and get me to the hospital, I will have this baby right here in the front seat of your precious Blue Ice. If you don't want to see that happen, I suggest you press on the gas and get me to the hospital."

This car is fully electric, Marcellous thought, so there was no gas to push. However, he decided in the name of self-preservation he would be better off keeping that to himself.

The couple was now only a few moments from the hospital, and the nurses would then be able to take over and he would be able to breathe again.

"No worries, babe," Marcellous said in a calm, reassuring voice as he reached his hand over to his wife's hand. "We are almost there."

"Don't you touch me." The words came in rapid succession. "Oh...the pain. Get this baby out of me. And why is it so hot? Turn on the air. You are roasting me to death. Me and the baby. Is that your plan? To make us bake in the car while you take your sweet time getting me to the hospital?"

Marcellous shook his head in disbelief. Though he knew this wasn't truly his sweet wife talking, he still felt himself holding his tongue from his natural inclination to retort. Nine months of pregnancy had turned into nine months and two weeks and those extra two weeks had Jasmyn at her wits' end.

Saved by the bell, he thought as he turned into the hospital and saw a nurse standing outside the entrance with a wheelchair holding a sign that read, "Thompson." That was a new one. He'd had no idea that they offered curbside service.

When Jasmyn began to feel continuous contractions, she was convinced that the baby could come at any moment. Marcellous contacted the hospital, and they said that her OB-GYN, Dr. Prince, could not be located at the time but that they would let her know that the Thompson's were on their way to the hospital. They also contacted the on-call doctor as a backup.

Marcellous depressed the brake, reached over to the touchscreen, and pressed the unlock icon to unlock the door. While the nurse began to help Mrs. Thompson exit the vehicle, Marcellous hopped out of the driver's side.

"Oh, thank you so much for being out here and ready to take her inside. Wait. Let me grab her bag and we will be all set to go."

"No worries, Mr. Thompson," the nurse said with a genuine smile, "We will take great care of your wife. Why don't you go park the car, grab the bag, and then come on in when you're done? We will take her up to labor and delivery located on the fifth floor. You can meet us there."

"Oh right, the car. OK. I will go park the car and then come up to labor and delivery on the fourth floor."

"Fifth floor, Mr. Thompson."

"My bad! Fifth floor. Gotcha."

Marcellous took another look at his wife and thought to himself how utterly beautiful she was and how much he truly loved her. Reading his mind, Jasmyn looked at him with a smile plastered on her face and said, "I love you, Marcellous."

He looked back at his wife and said, "I love you too, Jasmyn. I'll go park the car and then be right back." He watched the nurse wheel his wife toward the sliding doors as he settled back into the driver's seat.

As he pulled away from the hospital door to find a parking spot, his phone rang. It was Donatella, the baby's soon to be Godmother and a special agent with the Federal Bureau of Investigations.

He answered the phone feeling more at ease now that the professionals had his wife, and they would ensure their first child would make it into the world safe and sound. "Hey Donatella, I was just about to call you. We –"

"Marcellous, are you still with Jasmyn?" she interrupted Marcellous in a huff. "Are you at the hospital?"

Alarms began to register in his head. "No, I'm not with her. I just dropped her off with the nurse at the entrance to the hospital. They are taking her up to labor and delivery."

"Shit!" she said in a panicked voice. "This has all been a trap. A well-orchestrated trap. Jasmyn is in dire danger and you need to find her immediately."

Marcellous, beginning to process that his wife could be in mortal danger, quickly rotated the steering wheel a full 180 degrees, pressed the accelerator and quickly made his way back to the entrance. Without taking any time to place the car in park, he opened the door and ran inside. He frantically scanned the lobby and didn't see his wife, but his eyes connected with a nurse who was eyeing him. The nurse began to approach Marcellous.

"You must be Marcellous. I was told to expect you and your wife. Is she outside in the car?"

"What do you mean, is she in the car? I just dropped her off with a nurse who was waiting outside," he stated in a confused voice.

"Waiting outside?" the nurse stated, raising an eyebrow. "I only received the call mere minutes ago and I haven't had time to tell anyone else. I came right down so I could meet you both."

With panic in his voice, he raised the phone back to his ear, "Donatella, they've got her. They've got Jasmyn."

BUY BOOK #2, *Hour of Reckoning,* to find out who has taken Jasmyn and how Donatella will get her back!

This book is a work of fiction. Names, characters, places or incidents are products of the author's imagination and are used fictitiously. Any resemblance to actual events or persons, living or dead, is entirely coincidental.

Driftwood Springs

Copyright © 2020 by Shadow World Productions, LTD. All rights reserved. No part of this book may be reproduced in any form, except for the inclusion of brief quotations in a review, without permission in writing from the author or publisher

The scanning, uploading, and distribution of this book without written permission is a theft of the authors' intellectual property. If you would like to use materials from this book (other than for review purposes), prior written permission must be obtained by contacting the publisher at permissions@shadowworldproductions.com. Thank you for your support of the authors' rights.

First edition: April 2020

ISBN 978-0-9771133-1-6 (paperback)

ISBN 978-0-9771133-2-3 (hardcover)

❦ Created with Vellum

Made in the USA
Coppell, TX
09 April 2024

31112673R00152